Releasing his collar, Lola planted her palms on his chest and pushed, wrenching her mouth away from his. A foot of space now separated them, but their gazes remained locked.

Lola steeled herself against the obviously practiced look of surprise on his face. It didn't matter how great of a kisser he was or that he had a body that would play a starring role in her fantasies for nights to come. She wasn't about to give *Celebrity Pranks* the satisfaction or video footage of her looking like she was falling for a stripper.

Time to take back the control she'd momentarily lost along with her damned mind. *Take this,* Celebrity Pranks, she thought. She rounded the police chief and with her good hand, smacked him soundly on the butt.

"Now take off your clothes and dance!"

The sound of female laughter drew Lola's attention to the doorway of the waiting room. The nurse she'd met earlier leaned against the doorjamb with her arms folded over her chest. "Now that's a sight I'd like to see myself." Avis winked. "I see you've gotten acquainted with our chief of police."

Lola's jaw dropped.

"P-police chief?" she croaked, hoping she'd heard the woman wrong.

"Yes, police chief." The deep baritone of the man she'd assumed was a stripper rumbled behind her, confirming the fact that she'd really screwed up this time.

Dear Reader,

We've all seen them. Wild, wonderful, spirited women who were tamed by the love of a good man. Some call it growing up. I call it a shame.

It got me to thinking what-if?

What if the youngest of the Espresso Empire siblings, Lola Gray, didn't change? What if her impulsiveness and over-the-top ways, which usually land her in a hot mess, became an asset? What if she met a man wise enough to realize the things everyone around Lola considers faults are actually her greatest strengths?

Small-town police chief Dylan Cooper was the hunky answer to all my questions. And as he works to help get Lola out of a jam and out of town, he realizes she's the spark both his life and the town lacked—and nobody wants her to change or leave.

I hope you enjoy Lola's story, which concludes the Espresso Empire series.

All my best,

Phyllis

Heated Moments

PHYLLIS BOURNE

HARLEQUIN® KIMANI™ ROMANCE

ISBN-13: 978-0-373-86431-7

Heated Moments

For questions and comments about the quality of this book please contact us at CustomerService@Harlequin.com.

Printed in U.S.A.

A former newspaper crime reporter, **Phyllis Bourne** writes romantic comedy to support her lipstick addiction. A two-time Romance Writer's of America Golden Heart finalist, she has also been nominated for an RT Reviewer's Choice Best Book Award and won the Georgia Romance Writer's Maggie Award of Excellence. When she's not at her computer, Phyllis can be found at a cosmetics counter spending the grocery money.

Books by Phyllis Bourne

Harlequin Kimani Romance

Taste for Temptation
Sweeter Temptation
Every Road to You
Falling into Forever
Moonlight Kisses
Heated Moments

Visit the Author Profile page at
Harlequin.com for more titles.

For Mom and Elizabeth, and authors Farrah Rochon, Michelle Monkou and Patricia Sargeant.

And as always, for Byron, you are my heart, and every day with you is a real-life romance novel.

Chapter 1

"Son of a...!"

An uncharacteristic censuring glare from her father halted Lola Gray's curse, but not her outrage. She glared at her family gathered in the boardroom of Espresso Cosmetics for their quarterly meeting.

"Calm down, baby girl," her stepbrother and company CEO, Cole Sinclair, warned from the head of the conference room table. The endearment didn't diminish the sting of his stern tone. Nor did it soften the blow of him using against her the voting rights she had entrusted him with.

"Calm down?" Lola asked, incredulous. Standing abruptly, she flung a head shot of the model they intended to replace her with across the boardroom table. "How would you feel if I gave your job to a drag queen?"

"That drag queen was nearly your new step-mother." The gravelly voice of Espresso's longtime secretary, Loretta Walker, chimed in.

A grunt sounded from Lola's father's direction. "Are you ever going to let that go?"

"Not as long as I'm still breathing," Loretta retorted.

"It was an honest mistake," Lola's father grumbled. "The guy looked just like a woman, a *really good-looking* one."

Lola's shoulder-length hair swished against her shoulders as her head swiveled between them like a tennis ball in a championship match between Venus and Serena.

Unbelievable.

She'd walked through the doors of the Espresso building this morning expecting to hear an update on their family business, as well as more information about her upcoming photo shoot in China for the new red-lipstick collection. Instead, her family had broken the news she was out as the face of Espresso, as casually as they'd poured coffee from the carafe situated at the center of the long table.

And now they'd segued to an entirely different topic.

"Gorgeous, isn't he?" Lola's older sister, Tia Gray-Wright picked up the discarded glossy photo. "This was the most challenging makeover I've ever done, but Freddy Finch is one stunning woman…uh, I mean man…um, I mean…"

Her husband and now Espresso's attorney, Ethan Wright, patted his wife's hand. "We know what you mean, sweetheart, and you did a spectacular job." He turned to his father-in-law. "Always check the neck, man."

Cole nodded in agreement. "And if you spot a giant Adam's apple bobbing in the throat, then *she* is more than likely a *he*."

Raucous laughter erupted around the table. Lola stared at them openmouthed. If she didn't know better, she'd think she was in the middle of a comedy-club act instead of a business meeting.

How could they all sit around joking after the bomb they'd just dropped?

Fed up, Lola fisted her hands on hip bones sharpened by years of torturous exercise and a diet of tasteless protein shakes. "Shut up!" she yelled. "Every one of you. Just shut up!"

Silence fell upon the room, and the startled eyes of its occupants landed on her. Satisfied she finally had her attention, Lola wanted to make it crystal clear she wasn't going to stand by and let them take her job. Not without a fight.

"As a member of this family and a part owner of Espresso Cosmetics, I have a say in this matter," she began.

"I hold your proxy," Cole reminded her. Again, his chilly monotone had a firm edge, so different than the indulging one he'd always used with her. "So you've already had your say."

"That was fine when I was out of the country for months at a time, but I'm back now. I'll vote my own shares, thank you very much. We'll just do a recount."

Lola turned imploring eyes to Cole's new wife, Sage, who had recently merged her own cosmetics company with Espresso. Her sister-in-law had a rebellious streak. If she got Sage on her side, Lola calculated quickly, and then sweet-talked her father into changing his mind, she'd have the voting power to overturn Cole's decision to oust her as the face of Espresso Cosmetics.

Sage glanced at her husband, and Cole winked in response. Lola's hopes plummeted as she watched her sister-in-law's light brown face flush. She recognized a dick-whipped woman when she saw one, and Sage was clearly under his spell. Just as she expected, her sister-in-law shook her head slowly and mouthed the word *no*.

Cole cleared his throat. "Even if you did vote your shares, it's not enough to overrule my decision," he said. "Mr. Freddy Finch is the new face of Espresso Cosmetics. We'll announce it to the public next month. He'll also travel to Hong Kong to shoot the campaign for the special-edition red lipsticks."

"So this was a done deal before I even walked into the building," Lola whispered, more to herself than to them. "I never stood a chance."

She glanced around the room at her father, siblings and their spouses. Her family. They were the very people who were supposed to have her back. Instead, she felt their disloyalty as keenly as if they'd took turns plunging a knife into her back.

"I have a contract. I'll sue." Lola knew she was grasping.

"That wouldn't be wise," Ethan said, sounding more like the lawyer he was than her brother-in-law.

Cole heaved a sigh from the head of the table. "Hopefully that's settled." He turned to his secretary. "What's next on the agenda?"

"It is certainly not settled." Lola struggled to keep her emotions in check. "This—this is…" she stammered, her brain scrambling for the right word. "This is bullshit!"

"Lola!" her father admonished from the other end of the conference table.

However, she had too much at stake to back down. "You raised me to call it as I see it, and that's exactly what I'm going to do." She addressed her father, and then scanned the room.

"I put my best face forward for years, while this company churned out one stale collection after another, earning the reputation as old-lady makeup," Lola argued. She was the one the public associated with Espresso's senior-citizen image. Not her in-laws, her father or her siblings. "Now that we're finally making a comeback with fresh colors and exciting new products, you want to kick me to the curb, for a man in a wig."

Zeroing in on her brother, Lola jabbed a gel-manicured fingertip in his direction. "If that's not a load of crap, then you tell me what is!"

Cole raised a brow. "Since you never have a problem saying exactly what's on your mind, I'll return the favor." His eyes narrowed as he leaned back in the black leather executive chair. "Let's start with this sudden concern for your job. Where was it last year when Tia had to personally escort you to the airport so you could make a flight to a location shoot?"

He fired off another question before Lola could answer the first one. "Do you know how much it cost Espresso to appease that prima donna photographer you kept waiting?"

She knew before she opened her mouth to explain that he wouldn't understand. Her sister certainly hadn't. "My very best friend's fiancé had just called off their engagement, a week before their wedding. Britt was hysterical. How could I walk away when she needed me most?"

"Easy," Cole said. He appeared as unmoved as Tia had been at the time. "You hand her a box of tissues and head for the door."

Lola closed her eyes briefly and wondered how she could be from the same family as her coldhearted older siblings. Then she remembered, when it came to Espresso, their late mother and company founder, Selina Sinclair Gray, could be downright brutal.

Cole wasn't finished. "Then, following that hotel incident where you were kicked out after throwing a wild party and trashing their suite, I specifically cautioned you to stay out of trouble, but instead of heed-ing my warning you made news again. What was it this time?" He turned to his secretary, who was all too eager to supply him with an answer. "That's right, last week an airplane en route to Nashville from Los Angeles had to make a pit stop in Denver, so you could be hauled off it for allegedly assaulting a fellow passenger."

"B-but—" Lola began.

Again, her brother barely let her utter a word in her own defense. "Do you know how embarrassing it was for Espresso to have its top representative escorted off an airplane by security? Cell-phone videos of it went viral. You're still all over the internet, dragging our company down with you."

His secretary held up her tablet computer. "Lola's airline fiasco is currently trending higher on social media than those reality-show sisters with the big behinds," she said.

Lola rolled her eyes. So much for hoping the hubbub would die down. The wisecracks about her on celebrity gossip websites and YouTube snippets replayed in her head. Even worse, tabloid television shows had run different cell-phone videos of the same incident every night since it happened, adding horrid titles such as Espresso Diva's Mile High Tantrum and Pretty Ugly: Lola Attacks Man over Smelly Feet.

Of course, there had been no video footage of the uncouth passenger in the row behind her resting his bare feet atop the seat—and the head—of the elderly gentleman sitting beside her.

Lola exhaled. Contrary to what Cole believed, she

had taken his warning seriously, and she had *really, really* tried not to intervene, knowing the last thing she needed was more trouble.

She'd white-knuckled the armrests as the jerk behind them blatantly disregarded the flight attendant's repeated requests to put his feet on the floor where they belonged. *"It's none of your business."* Lola remembered muttering the words under her breath almost like a mantra.

However, when her senior-citizen seatmate's polite pleas were met with the oaf behind them laughing and wiggling his toes, impulse took over. She'd jumped from her seat and shoved the offending feet off the elderly man's chair, earning the grandfather's heartfelt gratitude and the applause of everyone in the first-class cabin.

Unfortunately, the moment the lout had caught sight of her famous face he'd immediately yelped in pain and crumpled into the fetal position.

The upshot: they were both escorted off the plane. Lola was flanked by security, while the rude passenger, who claimed she'd beaten him senseless, was hauled away in a wheelchair, his contrived moans and groans echoing in the air.

"Your behavior was unacceptable," Cole said.

"But they got the story all wrong," Lola said. By the time airport security got to the truth and released her with an apology, the strangers taking videos on their cell phones were long gone. "I was simply helping a fellow passenger."

Tia shook her head. Lola saw her father stifle a

yawn with his fist, and her brother-in-law took a surreptitious glance at his watch.

"You also helped yourself right out of representing Espresso," Cole said.

"Under the circumstances, any of you would have reacted the exact same way," Lola countered. "Only no one else would be painted as a volatile diva or have to stand here pleading for their job." Nor would they have to dodge tabloid television reporters trying to goad them into saying or doing something stupid.

Cole rubbed a hand over his close-cropped hair. He met her gaze, and for a moment, Lola thought she'd actually gotten through to him.

"My decision stands," he said finally.

"B-but—"

"The subject is closed."

"So where does this leave me?" Years of practice kept her posture ramrod straight, but Lola couldn't control the telltale quiver in her voice as she looked around the table. "Or did you all go behind my back and vote me out of this family, too?"

"Of course not, baby girl." Her father's face, which like Cole's had been uncharacteristically hard, softened with his tone.

"You know better," Tia said.

Lola raised a brow. "Do I?"

Cole cleared his throat, loudly. "We discussed this earlier," he said, his words aimed at Tia and their father. "Lola's not a child anymore. She's a twenty-five-year-old woman." He continued as if she wasn't standing right in front of them. "And these situations, incidents, or whatever you want to call the messes her impulsiveness constantly gets her into, are bad for business."

Realization dawned as Lola studied her siblings, who had both married over the past year and a half, and their spouses.

"Oh, now I see where this is going." Maybe she hadn't been booted from the family yet, Lola thought, but they were definitely ganging up on her. She pointed at her sister and brother-in-law. "First, there's you two, who are so in sync you finish each other's sentences." Then she turned to her brother and Sage. "Next we have the two of you, who are so much alike, it's downright scary."

Cole huffed out an impatient sigh. "What's that got to do with anything?"

"It appears I'm the odd man out, in this family as well as this company."

Her brother frowned. "Look, we have a lot of Espresso business to cover, including our plans for the building, dealing with competition from Force Cosmetics and future ad campaigns for Freddy," he said. "So either have a seat and put that marketing degree you earned online to work, or stop holding us up with this ridiculousness."

"R-ridiculousness?" she stammered.

Ignoring her protests, Cole signaled his secretary who announced the next item on the meeting agenda.

A discussion about the future of Espresso's aging building ensued. Meanwhile, Lola stood frozen, dazed from the callousness of her so-called loved ones. They'd actually pulled the plug on her career, she thought. A career that had already been on life support.

The New York City–based talent agency Lola had hired to field offers outside of Espresso hadn't taken her calls since the amateur videos of the airplane incident became social-media fodder. Not that they had presented her with a job she'd actually consider.

Lola wasn't sure how long she'd been standing there when the sound of Cole calling her name yanked her out of her own head.

"Well, are you going to just pose like a mannequin, or help us strategize next year's ad campaigns for your replacement?" he asked.

She blinked. After leading their family's underhanded coup, her brother had the unmitigated gall to expect her help. There was no way in hell she'd take him up on his offer. She opened her mouth to tell him so.

Don't be hasty.

A warning from her inner voice, the same one that tried so hard to keep her impulsiveness and tendency to say exactly what was on her mind from getting her into trouble, made Lola hesitate.

You may not like it, but it's the best offer you've had in months.

Lola recalled the proposed gigs the talent agency had called with, and cringed. But how could she even consider her family's offer after the way they'd all treated her this morning, not to mention the humiliation of being replaced by a drag queen?

Swallow your pride and take the job!

"We're all eager to hear your thoughts," her sister said encouragingly.

Gulping, Lola tried to swallow the lump of indignation stuck in her throat. "I—I…" she began.

It just wouldn't go down.

"Well?" Cole asked. "Surely, as Espresso's *former* model you have something useful to say."

Glaring at her brother, Lola silently told her inner voice to take a hike, along with any notions of kowtowing to the very people who had just given her the boot. "All I have to tell y'all is where to shove the idea of me helping you screw me over."

"Lola—" her brother began, but this time she was the one to interrupt.

"I'll give you a hint." She looked pointedly at the chairs under their behinds. "You're sitting on it."

Without stopping to think about her actions or the consequences of them, she hefted her pink leather tote off the table and walked toward the open conference room door. Lola paused in the doorway and glanced over her shoulder.

"Firing me was a huge mistake," she said. "I'll try to remember we're family when you all come crawling for me to save this company and your asses."

Pulling the sunglasses perched on her head down to cover her eyes, Lola strutted down the hallway toward the bank of elevators, reveling in the stupefied expressions on their faces.

She jabbed the down button and flipped her hair over her shoulder, noting the frayed ends. Espresso wasn't the only cosmetic company in the world, she told herself. Once word got out she was available, there would be plenty of offers from rival brands.

"Wait!" A male voice rang out as she boarded the elevator.

Humph. It didn't take them long to realize they'd screwed up in letting her go. Lola pressed her lips together to stifle a grin. Triumphant, she spun around, only to see not a member of her family, but one of the building's maintenance crew carrying a ladder.

"Thanks for holding the elevator, Miss Gray."

Remembering the employee was a newlywed, Lola inquired about his wife on the ride down to the lobby. Making small talk kept her mind off the fact that the sense of satisfaction she'd gleaned from her parting shot at her family had diminished. So had her confidence she'd ever be offered another job as good as the one she'd just lost.

In reality, with the exception of some runway work during New York and European Fashion Weeks, there was only one segment of the market vying for her face. At her age, a very unappealing market.

The elevator pinged.

"See you around, Miss Gray," the coverall-clad worker said.

Putting one foot in front of the other, Lola walked in the direction of the building's exit with her head held high, as her insides began to cave over the morning's events.

She stopped short when she spotted through the lobby windows a man she'd recognized. He was standing in front of the parking garage across the street. The slimeball was a cameraman for the reality show *Celebrity Pranks*, and he appeared to be in deep conversation with a guy dressed in a clown costume.

Lola bit back a curse. That stupid show had been out to trip her up since the airplane incident. She'd first seen the cameraman lurking outside a boutique in Atlanta three days ago, only that time his partner had been dressed in a gorilla costume. Fortunately, another shopper had come in and mentioned a *Celebrity Pranks* SUV parked around the corner.

It would serve them right if she marched across the street, snatched the big red nose off that clown and stuck it...

"Oh, no, you don't," Lola muttered, this time allowing the voice of common sense to overrule her impulse.

Unemployed or not, the last thing she needed was to be caught on video getting in that clown's painted face. The footage would fuel the reality show's ratings better than any stupid prank they had up their sleeve to make a fool out of her.

Lola continued to watch them through the lobby's floor-to-ceiling windows, debating whether to have Espresso's building security escort her to her car in the parking garage. Maybe she should just tuck her hair under the baseball cap in her bag and try to slip past them unnoticed.

Her phone buzzed, and she shrugged the massive designer tote off her shoulder. Rifling through it, Lola unearthed a curling iron, packets of protein-shake mix, a plastic blender bottle and the remote control for her television that had somehow made its way into the black hole of a bag. The ringing had stopped by the time she'd retrieved the phone, nearly nicking her fingers on a pair of scissors she'd used to cut crochet braids from her hair a few weeks ago.

Lola swiped the screen with her thumb. Her tote weighed down the crook of her arm like a bowling-ball bag. She listened to the message, gave the phone a quizzical glance and then frowned.

Her agent, Jill, had said it was urgent she return the call, but not much else.

"Lola, honey." Jill bubbled enthusiastically through the phone moments later. That saccharine-sweet voice laced with faux cheer could mean only one thing, Lola thought. She stifled a grunt. *Here we go.* Another offer to advertise something aimed at the AARP crowd.

"You won't believe who just called. They want you to—" Jill started.

"No." Lola cut her off. Usually, she would have heard the agent out and then politely declined, but after getting shafted by her family in the company boardroom and being stalked by that silly tabloid show already today she was in no mood.

"But you haven't even heard what the job is…"

Rolling her eyes, Lola tapped her foot against the lobby floor. She had a pretty good idea. Espresso's senior-citizen image clung to her, and no one seemed to care that she was only in her twenties.

"Look, I thought I already made this clear. I'm not

interested in being the face of a denture adhesive, walk-in bathtubs or doing commercials where I'm snuggled up to some old dude with an idiotic grin on my face because he popped a pill to get a hard-on."

"I promise, this one is different. It's a fantastic opportunity and absolutely perfect for you," Jill insisted.

Lola grunted again. "Yeah, I've heard that before."

"Please. Just hear me out."

Lola shrugged. At this point, she had nothing to lose by listening. She leaned against the wall near the windows and faced the lobby's interior. "Fine, go ahead."

The agent filled her in on the details, and Lola broke out in a huge grin. If she played her cards right, this wouldn't be just a job, but the opportunity of a lifetime.

She ended the call and dropped the phone into her pit of a bag.

"Boo-yah!" Pumping a fist in the air, she whispered the words she wanted to scream loudly enough for her family to hear on the tenth floor.

"I'm back!"

Nothing could bring her down now, Lola thought. Not even the sight of the maintenance worker from the elevator removing the giant poster of her that had hung from the lobby's rafters for years, and replacing it with one of a man wearing a blond wig and lipstick.

Chapter 2

Police Chief Dylan Cooper hadn't seen faces this unimpressed with what he had to say since dealing with his ex-wife.

"I hauled ten bad guys to jail last night," someone yelled from the back of the room. "Didn't even have to call for backup."

"Is that all?" A snort accompanied the shouted question. "I made over fifty arrests this week, including Big Moe, from the top of the most-wanted list."

Murmurs of approval echoed off the walls at the capture of the elusive Big Moe. They fueled the fervent bragging, each person who chimed in boasting bigger arrest statistics than the last.

"What about you, Chief? How many bad guys you take off the streets this week?"

Dylan had hauled the Henderson brothers to the county jail after they'd started a brawl at the sports bar to avoid making good on a wager. His efforts had earned him a sucker punch to the jaw from one of the lumberjack-sized brothers, while he'd been busy subduing the other two.

However, those arrests had been two weeks ago.

The metallic gleam of the badge pinned to his uniform caught Dylan's eye as he glanced at the worn carpet. He raised his head slightly to meet the dozens of expectant faces awaiting his reply.

"None," he said finally.

A chorus of gasps erupted, quickly followed by muffled giggles.

"However," Dylan interjected over the din, "I run a small-town police department, not a video game controller." He eyed the classroom of fourth and fifth grade Cooper's Place Elementary School students gathered for his day-in-the-life career talk. "So those arrests you all made playing Cop Crackdown don't count."

"Not even nabbing Big Moe?" the boy in the back of the room asked.

Dylan took a moment to think it over. A few of his cop buddies back at his old precinct in Chicago played the popular video game, but none had managed to beat the last level and capture the slippery Big Moe.

Dylan stroked the shadow of beard clinging to his chin. "Well, maybe…"

"Dylan Cooper." The sound of his name, spoken in an admonishing tone he rarely heard, grabbed his attention. He turned from the students seated crosslegged on the floor to their teacher standing in a corner of the classroom with her arms folded over her chest.

"Yes, Mrs. Bartlett." Dylan's deep voice automatically adopted the singsong quality it had decades ago when she'd been his fifth-grade teacher.

She peered at him over the frames of cat-eye glasses that had slid past the bridge of her nose. Her lips were pursed into a frown, deepening the wrinkles around her mouth. Time had transformed the teacher's once dark hair to salt and pepper. However, her expression was the same she'd worn the day a garter snake he'd encountered on the way to school had escaped his backpack and slithered onto her desk.

"These students are in my classroom on this sunny July day because they spent the school year trying to apprehend Big Moe instead of doing their homework." She paused and gave the open window a pointed glance. As if on cue, the happy shrieks of children at the small town's playground floated in on the mild breeze.

Dylan exhaled, shoving aside a twinge of empathy for the kids' plight. It didn't matter that he'd once missed a summer of Little League baseball sitting in this same classroom, with the same teacher. He was the adult now as well as an authority figure.

"No," he said finally. "Nabbing Big Moe doesn't count as a real arrest."

Mrs. Bartlett rewarded the statement with an approving smile. But if the grumbles filling Dylan's ears were any indication, his stock had dropped even further with his audience.

"Isn't it your job to arrest people?" a kid seated in front asked. "That's what the police do."

"Not always," Dylan replied. "My main duty is to keep everyone safe. In a town the size of ours that could mean anything from teaching you bicycle safety to helping Devon's grandmother across Main Street." He inclined his head toward one of the boys and then looked over at a set of identical twins. "Or even helping Natalie and Nicole look for their lost puppy."

Dylan acknowledged the waving hand of a boy he recognized as an old high school classmate's son. "Got a question, Ryan?"

"Where's your gun?" the boy asked.

"At home," Dylan replied. "I'm not on duty today. Besides, weapons don't belong in a classroom. I didn't bring one here today, and you should never, ever bring a gun or anything else that could be potentially dangerous to school either, right?"

Heads in the audience bobbed in agreement, and then he saw one kid raise his hand.

Dylan looked down at him. "What is it, Brandon?"

"Is a Swiss Army knife okay? I got one for my birthday. It's so cool, I wanted to show all my friends." The kid held out his hand. A shiny red utility knife rested in his small upturned palm.

"That is a very cool present. However, it's not appropriate to bring it to school." Dylan remembered having one just like it when he was the kid's age. However, times had changed. "I don't want you to get into trouble, so how about you give it to me for now. I'll give it to your dad later, and he'll return it to you."

Dylan pocketed the small knife and stole a glance at the clock on the back wall. Although this was one of his rare days off, he had a meeting this afternoon at city hall about the upcoming mayoral election.

"Well, kids, from my early-morning drive around town to check out everything to my night rounds and beyond, that's a typical day in the life of a small-town police chief," he concluded.

"Sounds boring to me, Chief. Just like this hick town," the boy who'd caught Big Moe yelled. "I can't wait until I'm old enough to move away and live someplace fun."

Another boy chimed in. "Me, too. When I grow up, I'm going to be a real cop like the ones on my mom's favorite show, *Law & Order*, not hanging around here helping old ladies cross the street."

Dylan took in stride the comments and ridiculing snickers that followed. After all, he'd felt the exact same way when he was their age. He'd also done exactly what they intended to do. The moment he graduated high school, he'd fled the town named for his ancestors, with big plans and his high school sweetheart on his arm.

He'd never planned to return to Cooper's Place, but he was back in his hometown doing a job that most days held all the excitement of watching grass grow. Slowly. One blade at a time.

Still, dull was good, he reminded himself.

His stint as a beat cop and then two years as a homicide detective on Chicago's south side had given him an appreciation for living in a place where the children he heard outside could play without fears of gunshots ringing out. Sure, he went on routine calls concerning shoplifters, noise disturbances, family and neighbor disputes, and the occasional burglary. However, there were no calls in the middle of the night to investigate homicides. No street gangs or armed robberies.

The biggest thing a person was likely to become a victim of here was local gossip.

Cooper's Place, Ohio, was still a town where the residents were all on a first-name basis and could go to bed at night without double-checking to see if the doors were locked. Peace and quiet reigned here, and Dylan would do everything in his power to keep it that way.

After answering a few more questions, he eyed the exit sign above the classroom door. "It's been a pleasure speaking with you today," he said.

His former teacher gave the students a reading assignment and followed him into the corridor. "I'd like to have a word with you, Chief Cooper," she said, closing the classroom door behind her.

Dylan groaned inwardly at the use of his title, hoping she wasn't about to give him an update on her ongoing dispute with her next-door neighbor. He'd issued them both citations last month when they'd insisted on pursuing charges against one another over minor transgressions that should have been settled without police involvement.

"How can I help?" he asked.

"It's that uncle of yours." She frowned. "My case was heard in Mayor's Court last week…"

He held up a hand to stop her. Cooper's Place was one of the small Ohio municipalities that had established Mayor's Court to hear small cases that would be decided by arbitration. Since the mayor held a law degree, he was qualified to oversee the proceedings. Unfortunately, residents unhappy with the decisions made there often voiced their displeasure to Dylan.

"I'm law enforcement, Mrs. Bartlett. I have no control over Mayor's Court or the mayor's rulings. If you don't agree with his decision you can always appeal to the county court."

"But he's *your* family," she said.

"Regardless, any problems you have with the way he does his job should be taken up with him or at the ballot box during the upcoming election."

"Humph," she muttered. "How can I vote against him if he always runs unopposed?"

Moments later, Dylan stood outside the elementary school building and pulled his mobile phone from his shirt pocket. He briefly debated whether to check in with Dispatch.

The two-man department's second officer was on duty today, and although Dylan couldn't have asked for a more dedicated employee, Todd Wilson still had less than a year of experience under his belt.

Also, the rookie could be a bit of a zealot in making sure the town's citizens adhered to the exact letter of the law, handing out citations to jaywalkers and litterbugs. Wilson sometimes carried a ruler to measure how far drivers had parked from the curb, and then slapped a ticket on their windshields if a quarter of an inch put them in violation.

The young man's fanatical devotion to the job combined with his clumsy nature often made him the butt of jokes, and the good folks of Cooper's Place teased the guy mercilessly. Some even compared him to the bumbling deputy from a classic black-and-white television show.

Holding the phone to his ear, Dylan listened as it rang twice before the dispatcher answered.

"Quiet as usual, Chief," Marjorie Jackson said robotically, as if she'd been expecting his call. After all, he always checked in on the two days off he allowed himself each month. Dylan guessed he'd torn her away from one of the celebrity magazines she read constantly.

"And Wilson?" Dylan inquired.

"He drove the cruiser out to Old Mill Road to monitor for speeders."

Dylan briefly considered driving out there to tell the officer to stick closer to town, since the area around Old Mill Road had both spotty radio coverage and cell phone dead spots, but he decided against it. The dispatcher had already confirmed nothing was going on.

Traffic was practically nonexistent on Old Mill Road now that the new bypass had opened. Surrounded by cornfields, there was little chance of the young cop finding a speeder or getting into a situation he couldn't handle.

Exhaling, Dylan stared up at the sky and squinted against the beaming sun. He caught sight of a small dark cloud in the distance as he donned his wire-rimmed aviator shades, and despite the otherwise placid skies, he couldn't shake the feeling a storm was about to blow into town.

Chapter 3

Lola squirmed behind the wheel of her red Mustang.

After hours on the road, driving to New York City no longer seemed like the brilliant idea it had back in Nashville. Her shoulders ached and her butt had gone numb fifty miles ago.

She should have stopped to stretch at the last rest stop, on the Kentucky-Ohio border, Lola thought, massaging the kink in her neck. Instead she'd blown right past it, still buzzing with excitement over the offer her talent agency had presented to her earlier this morning.

America Live!

Lola stopped rubbing her neck long enough to give her driving arm a hard pinch.

Nope. It wasn't a dream.

In a few days, she'd actually be filling in as a temporary cohost on *America Live!* And the producers had indicated the one-day gig would also serve as her audition for a permanent spot on the top-rated morning show.

A smile formed on her lips as she imagined her family, especially her big brother, looking over the rims of their coffee mugs at their television screens Monday morning and seeing her. They'd be shocked, all right.

The same woman they'd cast aside would be looking back at them. Lola grinned harder. Too bad she wouldn't be able see the looks on their faces.

"Notoriety appears to have worked to your advantage this time," Jill had told her during the brief call. "This is your shot, Lola. I don't have to tell you how important it is for you to bring your A game. Look your best and wow that audience," she'd instructed, before ending the call with a warning. "Don't screw this up!"

Not a chance, Lola thought.

Erring on the side of caution, she'd opted to drive solo to New York rather than fly. She didn't want to inadvertently bump someone on a plane and end up falsely accused of beating the crap out of the person. Also, tabloid television shows tended to stake out airports to corner their prey. Now that she was on everybody's radar, she needed to lie low.

Still, one thing she hadn't been able to avoid was summer road construction. Her car's GPS system had instructed her to exit the interstate to follow detours on state and county roads. She stifled a yawn with her fist. Every mile seemed to take her deeper into the rural countryside. At least flanked by miles of Ohio farmland broken up with an occasional one-stoplight town, there was no way for her to find trouble *or for trouble to find her.*

The sound of her ringtone filled the Mustang's interior, and Lola snatched the cell phone off the passenger seat. She peeked at the number flashing across the screen and blew out a sigh.

Although it was Friday, she'd managed, while driving through Kentucky, to secure last-minute appointments in the city for an oxygen facial, brow wax and tint, and of course, a fresh manicure. Now she had to somehow persuade NYC's top stylist to work his cut-and-color magic on her lackluster mane over the weekend, so every head would turn to look at her when she entered the *America Live!* studio Monday morning.

"Pablo," Lola crooned into the phone. "I need a huge favor."

She'd briefly considered using the top-notch beauty team at her sister's flagship Espresso Sanctuary Spa before leaving Nashville, but she was too pissed at Tia to ask her for anything.

Besides, Pablo and Lola went way back, before he was known by just one name and had opened the exclusive salon with it emblazoned on the front door. She glanced at her split ends in the rearview mirror as she explained what she needed done to her hair.

"You should have called six months ago, babes,

because that's how far in advance I'm booked," Pablo said, a European accent lacing his words. "I'm only returning your call personally as a courtesy, because we're friends. However, I'm afraid what my receptionist told you earlier stands."

The stylist was her friend. That was why she decided to confide in him about her overall career situation and the humiliating way she'd been dumped as the face of Espresso. "So you can see how crucial it is that you do my hair and not relegate me to your assistant." Lola's voice cracked as she tried to persuade him to make an exception. "I've got a lot riding on this opportunity, Pablo. I need to look my best, which means I need you. *Please.*"

Long moments of silence ensued. Lola pressed her lips together and stared through the windshield at the endless ribbon of winding road, hoping he'd change his mind.

"Impossible," Pablo said, finally. "Not only do I not work on weekends, but I've been invited to an A-list celebrity party in the Hamptons. I'll be hanging there all weekend."

Lola wasn't giving up. "Nothing is impossible. Like when I insisted on you as my stylist for a magazine shoot, back when you were fresh out of cosmetology school and sweeping hair off Espresso Sanctuary's floor."

"I know you helped me out, Lola, but…"

"Not to mention floating you a loan to help you open your first salon in Nashville, when your loan applications were rejected by the both the bank and the small-business administration," she said. *"Remember?"*

She heard a sigh at the other end of the phone as she turned the steering wheel sharply to avoid hitting a squirrel that had darted out onto the road.

"Come on, Lola. We're talking the Hamptons here."

Lola frowned. She hadn't wanted to take it there, but he'd left her with no other option. "Be that way, *Sherman*." She emphasized his real name.

"You wouldn't." Pablo quickly lost his faux accent.

"What? Start a rumor that international stylist to the stars Pablo, who's led folks to believe he hails from Barcelona, is really Sherman Meeks from Shelbyville, Tennessee?"

"Don't you dare!" Pablo shrieked.

"Of course I wouldn't do that to you," she said in a syrupy-sweet tone as fake as "Pablo's" persona. "Besides, I'm sure your A-list friends and high-profile clients already know the *real* you."

"All right, you win," the stylist said in a huff. He rattled off a time on Sunday. "But you'd best be punctual, earlier if possible."

Lola glanced at the GPS, which estimated her time of arrival. She thanked her friend and assured him she'd be there.

"Good," Pablo said. "Otherwise, you'll be out of luck."

Lola tossed the phone back onto the passenger seat just as the GPS beeped. *Here we go again*, she thought.

"Accident ahead," the robotic voice warned. "Detouring to an alternative route."

Following its directions, Lola exited the state road. She steered the car along winding smaller roads that all seemed to lead deeper into nowhere.

"Turn left onto Old Mill Road."

She made the turn, and then noticed the gadget had recalculated her arrival time, adding another half hour to her journey. She also noticed a sign warning drivers to be on the lookout for cows in the road. The next sign took the speed limit down to forty-five miles an hour.

"At this rate, it'll take me a month to get there," Lola muttered.

Peering through the windshield, she didn't see any cows. In fact, she hadn't even encountered any other cars. Just a stretch of two-lane road cutting through acres of cornfields.

She nibbled on her bottom lip and shifted her gaze to the speedometer and then to the GPS's ever increasing arrival time. A life-changing career opportunity awaited her, and what was she doing? Slowpoking down back roads that looked like a corn maze, Lola thought.

The big toe of her driving foot twitched.

Giving in to the overwhelming impulse to floor it, she pressed the accelerator pedal. The muscle car lunged forward as the powerful engine roared its approval.

"This is more like it," Lola muttered, steering the car along the deserted road.

She didn't own a Mustang to drive it like the chauffeur in *Driving Miss Daisy*. The GPS took the faster speed into account and shaved ten minutes off her arrival time.

Lola switched on the sound system and the acerbic lyrics of Nicki Minaj poured through the car's speakers, filling the interior. With the afternoon sun on her face, Lola drummed out the fast, thumping beat with her fingertips against the steering wheel.

She saw the speedometer needle inch toward the seventy-five-miles-an-hour mark and then beyond. She was clocking eighty-five miles an hour when her killjoy of an inner voice reared its head, admonishing her to slow down.

The GPS shaved another twenty minutes off her estimated arrival to Manhattan. Lola scanned the windshield and then checked the side and rearview mirrors. No cows. No cars. Nothing but cornfields and open road. There was absolutely no reason for her not to make up some of the time that detours and delays had cost her.

She cranked up the radio and sang off tune in an off-key attempt to rap along with Nicki about being a badass.

A flash of blue lights caught her eye.

"No, no, no, no," Lola chanted, hoping it was just her imagination.

The wail of a siren drowned out the music. She spotted a police car in the side mirror, and her stomach did a free fall to the floorboards. She definitely wasn't imagining it. Maybe he wasn't after her, Lola thought, taking her foot off the accelerator. She saw a tractor in the distance plodding across a field.

Yeah, right, her inner voice scoffed.

Braking, Lola slowed the car enough to pull over to the side of the road. Her talent agent's warning about trouble and not to screw up played through her mind as she moved the gearshift into the Park position.

Lola eyed the side view mirror and watched the officer get out of the police car. She rolled down her window and narrowed her eyes as he walked toward the Mustang. With his lanky build, awkward gait and uniform a size too big, he looked like a teenager playing cop.

He fumbled with a notebook before dropping it on the ground. When he bent over to retrieve it, his hat fell off. She shook her head at the sight of him trying to get himself together. If she weren't facing what would undoubtedly be a pricey speeding ticket, she would have felt sorry for the guy.

"Afternoon, ma'am," he said, when he finally reached her car.

She removed her sunglasses. The officer blinked and then gawked at her, openmouthed. Lola was used to it. In a moment his face would register one of the looks she regularly got from strangers, recognition or, in the case of men, instant adoration.

She smiled, and his face flushed red. Yep, she thought, adoration.

"Officer." Lola looked at the name tag pinned to the shirt of the baggy uniform. "Officer Wilson."

The sound of his name appeared to snap him out of

his stupor. "Um…ma'am, do you realize how fast you were going?" His voice cracked, and he cleared his throat. "The posted speed limit on this road is forty-five miles an hour. I clocked you doing ninety-four."

Talking her way out of a ticket would be a chip shot, Lola thought. Feign ignorance, smile a lot and hit him with the facial expressions the camera loved.

Easy peasy.

You're in the wrong. Take the ticket and be on your way.

Lola sighed. Maybe it was time for her to finally allow that inner voice to take the wheel.

"Sorry, Officer," she said simply. No explanations. No excuses.

Her goal was to get to New York City as quickly and uneventfully as she could. Sitting here trying to sweet-talk her way out of a ticket would only delay her further, or even worse, get her into trouble she had gone out of her way to avoid.

The blush rose from Officer Wilson's neck to his thin face. "I'll need to see your driver's license and car registration." He fumbled with the pad in his hand, but this time he managed to hold on to it.

Leaning over, Lola opened the glove box and re-trieved a small plastic folder containing both her car registration and proof of insurance. She handed it to Officer Wilson, then winced as it slipped from his grasp.

While he looked over her registration, Lola hefted her designer tote from the floorboard of the pas-senger's side to the seat. Her arm muscles strained from the effort. Geez, she thought, if the thing got any heavier she'd have to put wheels on it and roll it around like a piece of luggage.

"Your registration is in order." Officer Wilson returned the plastic folder. "Driver's license, please."

"Just a sec." Lola stuck her hand inside the black hole of the oversize pink bag in search of her wallet. She rifled through the contents, unearthing a camera, next a flashlight and then a packet of protein powder.

One of these days she was going to have to clear out this bag, she thought, her arm elbow-deep in the mouth of the purse. She pulled out a small bottle of hand sanitizer and a pocket pack of tissues.

"Do you need help, ma'am?" The officer leaned down and peered through the open driver's side window.

"No, I got—" Pain sliced through her hand, and Lola yanked it from the bag. "Ow! Ow! Ow!"

Blood oozed from her palm and dripped down her arm. *Damn scissors*, she thought, looking at the wound. She should have pulled them from her bag weeks ago.

Lola glanced up at the officer, holding her bloody hand in her other one. "I know I have a first-aid kit somewhere in my purse. Maybe you could empty it and..."

The cop stepped back from the Mustang on wobbly legs, and the color drained from his face.

"Blood," he whispered, staring at her hand.

"It's just a little cut," Lola said, though it hurt like

hell. She positioned her arm to give him a better look. "See, it's not a big…"

His eyes rolled back in his head, and the poor guy looked as if he was about to drop on the spot.

"Officer Wilson," Lola yelled, throwing open the car door.

She reached out to steady him with her good hand, but was a second too late. He crumpled to the ground. Lola heard a horrifying thunk as the back of his head hit the gravel, cushioned only by weeds poking through.

"Shit! Shit! Shit!" Lola hissed.

Her cut forgotten, she knelt beside him.

"Officer Wilson?"

No response. She lifted his head to her knee and noted from the rise and fall of his chest that the cop was still breathing. *Thank God*, she thought, sending up a silent prayer. He didn't appear to be bleeding, but with her hand still dripping blood she couldn't be sure.

Grabbing the two-way radio from his belt, she pressed several of the buttons.

"Officer down," Lola yelled into it, imitating the lingo she'd heard on TV cop shows. But unlike television there was no reassuring voice saying the cavalry was coming to the rescue, only the hiss of dead air.

Closing her eyes briefly, she shoved aside the panic threatening to consume her.

"I'm just going to my car for my phone to call for help," Lola told the unconscious officer.

She rested the cop's head on the ground as gently as she could, and then dived inside her car. After snatching her cell phone off the passenger seat with trembling fingers, she hurriedly called 911.

Lola clutched the phone to her ear. Silence. She glanced at the screen. The words *No Service* had replaced the dots indicating signal strength.

The panic she'd banished was creeping up on her now. Looking down the barren road, she saw the tractor still inching through a field in the distance. It was too far away. She ran to the police car, hoping its radio would be more effective than the one the officer carried. Her efforts were rewarded with static and then more silence.

Returning to the unconscious cop's side, Lola exhaled a shaky breath. She had no idea if she should move him, but what choice did she have? She couldn't leave him here to go for help.

She was going to have to *take* him to help.

Lola rounded her car to the passenger's side and flung open the door. Back at the officer's side, she sucked in a deep breath before crouching on her haunches. She lifted his head and then his shoulders as gently as possible, finally managing to weave her arms under his.

The cop, who she would have described as scrawny when he'd stepped out of the patrol car earlier, was a lot heavier than he looked.

"Come on, Officer Wilson," she pleaded. "Help me out here."

Slowly, Lola dragged him across the hot pavement toward the passenger's side of her car. Rivulets of sweat rolled down her back as the sun beat on it, and for once she was grateful for years of torturous Pilates classes that had not only kept her lean, but made her strong.

Still, she was gasping for breath by the time she managed to get Officer Wilson slumped in the passenger's seat.

Back in the driver's seat, Lola snatched a wad of tissue from the pocket pack to stem the blood still oozing from her hand. She used her free hand to start a GPS search for the closest hospital.

"Hold on, Officer Wilson," she said, as the route to a facility a few miles away appeared. "I'll have you at Cooper's Place Community Hospital in a flash."

Chapter 4

A scowl and the smell of chocolate greeted Dylan as he stepped through the back door of his mother's house.

"When are you going to learn to knock before you barge into someone's home?" Virginia Cooper placed her hands on the floral apron covering her hips.

"Knock? I grew up in this house."

Standing at the stove, his mother jabbed a finger in his direction. "But the bills in the mailbox out front are in my name. I pay the cost to be the boss."

"Well, I definitely don't want to step on the boss's toes, especially when she's baking," Dylan conceded with a chuckle. The heavenly aroma coming from the oven appealed to his sweet tooth, prodding him to get off her bad side. "So, what's in the oven?"

A corner of his mother's mouth quirked upward in a hint of a smile, indicating he was out of the doghouse, at least for now. He doubted she'd still be smiling once she found out the reason behind his visit.

"White-chocolate-chip muffins." Virginia picked up a mechanical timer on the kitchen counter and turned the dial to set it. "They'll be ready in sixteen minutes. You staying?"

"I am now."

"Coffee?" she offered.

"Have a seat." Dylan gestured toward the high-back stools surrounding the large kitchen island, which was cleared except for his mother's closed laptop computer. When college football season started next month its smooth granite top would be loaded with a wide assortment of breakfast breads and his mother's homemade preserves. "You're providing homemade muffins. The least I can do is make coffee."

Virginia sat in one of the chairs while he opened the door to the cabinet where the coffee was kept.

"What's with the uniform? Thought you were finally taking a day off work."

Dylan dumped a scoop of coffee into a paper filter and placed it in the coffeemaker's brew basket. He added water and switched the machine on. While the coffee brewed, he rinsed the chocolate-muffin batter from the mixing bowl in the sink and placed it in the dishwasher.

"Technically, I am off, but I had a day-in-the-life career speech at the elementary school earlier. It's the students' last day of summer school." He glanced at his watch. "Right now I'm supposed to be at city hall. Uncle Roy called a department head meeting about the next mayoral inauguration, but it's been delayed. He's stuck in the waiting room at Doc Hadley's office, and the doc's running behind schedule."

"Inauguration? He hasn't even been reelected yet."

Dylan dried his hands with a paper towel. His late father's youngest brother had been mayor of the town named for their ancestors ever since Dylan could remember. "His reelection is pretty much a foregone conclusion. He wants to take the oath of office outdoors this time, in the town square, and wants it spruced up for the event."

"The town's budget is stretched enough. We can't afford the hours of overtime it would take for the public works department to work on the square." Virginia's snort filled the kitchen. "Besides, Roy's getting too damn old, not to mention crotchety, to hold office. He needs to hang it up. This town needs some fresh blood in the mayor's office."

Folding his arms, Dylan leaned against the kitchen counter. His snort was identical to his mother's. "There is no fresh blood. If nobody files to run in the next three weeks, he'll be running unopposed."

"Again," they both said, simultaneously.

His mother's eyes lit up. "You could run."

"No way." Dylan wagged a finger. "I'm not cut out to be a politician."

A gurgling sound emitted from the coffeemaker

indicated the end of the brewing cycle. Dylan crossed the room and retrieved two mugs from another cabinet.

He caught his mother's frown out of the corner of his eye. "Anyway, if you were mayor that would leave that bumbling Wilson boy as our new police chief, and that would really leave this town with something on our hands."

"Stop it, Mom," Dylan admonished. "He's young and a bit high-strung, but he tries hard and the job means everything to him."

Dylan sat the mugs on the kitchen island, filled them with coffee and then went to the refrigerator for the creamer.

"Humph. He gave me a twenty-dollar ticket for jaywalking on Main Street," Virginia said. "And I'm not the only one. I was with his great-grandmother, and he gave her one, too."

Dylan added a generous dollop of cream to his mother's mug and slid it toward her, leaving his black. Wilson was still a rookie and a stickler for every law on the books. His judgment on what he should probably turn a blind eye to—especially in a small town— would improve once he got more experience under his belt.

Meanwhile, Dylan supported his lone officer. "Were you two jaywalking?" he asked, standing across from her at the table.

"Yeah, but…"

He shrugged and eyed her over the rim of his mug. "Do the crime, pay the fine."

His mother harrumphed. "You'd think with practically everyone who runs this town having the last name of Cooper, I'd be able to get a ticket fixed," she grumbled, and then took a sip of coffee. "But your uncle Roy decided in Mayor's Court that we had to pay up. He even threatened us with a contempt-of-court charge when we voiced our displeasure with his decision, for, as he put it, 'mouthing off'."

The aroma of chocolate now thoroughly permeated the kitchen, pushing aside thoughts of his uncle. Dylan's stomach rumbled, reminding him he'd had only coffee and toast for breakfast, and his gaze wandered to the mechanical timer.

As if on cue, it dinged.

Virginia rose from her chair, walked over to the stove and switched off the timer. Donning oven mitts, she pulled the pan of muffins from the stove and placed it on a wire rack. She yanked off the mitts and returned to her coffee. "They need to cool for about five minutes."

"Nonsense." Dylan grabbed a dessert plate from the cabinet. He reached to pluck a muffin from the hot tin. Muffling a curse, he snatched his hand back and shook it.

"Greedy." Virginia laughed from her perch at the kitchen island.

Undeterred, he tried again, this time managing to get one onto his plate and barely singeing his hand. "Starving," he corrected.

Back at the table, Dylan took a huge bite out of the muffin and slowly chewed. The pleasant flavors of sugar, butter and cream that had won the woman seated across from him blue ribbons for baking at a decade of county fairs were notably absent. His taste buds revolted at the cruel trick his nose had played on them. He took a gulp of cooled coffee from his mug to put them out of their misery and wash the taste-less lump down.

He looked at his mother, who quickly averted her eyes. "What exactly was that?"

"A muffin, dear. I just made a few substitutions."

Standing at the coffeemaker, Dylan topped off his mug. "Like what? Swap out taste for dust?"

Virginia opened the lid of the laptop at her elbow. Pulling her reading glasses from her apron pocket, she peered through them at the screen. "I'm experimenting with some recipes to give my guests some healthier options next month," she said. "So I tweaked my regular muffin recipe a bit and cut the amount of sugar in half. I also substituted all-purpose flour with whole wheat flour, used applesauce instead of oil and mashed avocado instead of butter," she said.

Every autumn, the home Dylan had grown up in turned into a bed-and-breakfast and hosted fans and alumni of the college football team from a neighboring town. The four-room B and B was also the closest thing Cooper's Place had to a hotel.

"You might have warned me," he said.

His mother sighed as she typed with two fingers on the laptop. "I was going to take them to my garden club meeting and get their opinion, then you showed up," she said. "I thought I'd get your visceral reaction."

Dylan picked up his plate and slid the offending muffin in the trash can. "That visceral enough for you?"

"Maybe if I tried a mashed banana instead of the avocado," his mother said more to herself than to him, still staring at the screen.

"Just warn me next time," Dylan said.

Virginia looked up from the recipe, eyeing him over the rim of her glasses. "Speaking of which, what are you *really* doing here?"

Dylan exhaled. Crossing his arms, he leaned against the kitchen counter. "I was doing my morning patrol…"

"This is supposed to be your day off."

Dylan had still kept to his routine of doing an early-morning patrol around town before his officer came on duty. "Anyway, Rosemary Moody ran out of her hardware store and flagged down my truck," he continued.

"Hmmm." His mother pretended to be absorbed in the laptop, the telltale twitch of her left eye giving her away.

"She wanted to tell me your order had just come in, and she wanted to know when was a good time to deliver it."

Virginia shook her head. "That's what I get for doing business with the town blabbermouth," she grumbled. "I should have just driven to Columbus and picked up what I needed from Home Depot."

"Everybody blabs everyone else's business around here," Dylan said. It was a fact of small-town life he hadn't missed during his years in Chicago. "So, mind telling me what you intend to do with a truckload of concrete stones and concrete mix?"

He waited for an answer to his question, but her lips remained stubbornly pressed together.

"I'm going to find out eventually, so you might as well spill it."

She swiveled in her chair and faced him. "I want to put a fire pit out back. When the weather turns cool, the guests can sit out there and roast marshmallows, make s'mores."

"Sounds like a good idea," he said. "So I wonder why Luke didn't know anything about your plans when I asked him what was up?"

Dylan had his suspicions on why the bed-and-breakfast's part-time handyman was clueless, but wanted to hear the answer from his mother. He shifted his weight against the counter. Several moments passed. "You're not having that pit built, are you?"

She slowly shook her head.

"You were planning to try to do it yourself." Dylan chuckled. The sound was as dry as the muffin, which still left a bad taste in his mouth.

"Just hear me out, son." Virginia raised a hand. Without waiting on a response, she launched into a spiel about some television show on the Home Design channel called *Granny's Old House*, where a senior citizen tackles home improvement, design and landscaping projects.

Dylan listened as his mother babbled on, but only because he was waiting for her to stop long enough to take a breath. Then he could ask her if she was out of her flipping mind.

She tapped on the laptop's keyboard with her index fingers and then turned the screen toward him. "Granny says it'll only take a couple of hours." Virginia inclined her head toward the small screen. "See for yourself."

He glanced at the laptop. Sure enough, a woman with a hard hat covering her gray hair was on the business end of a shovel, talking about how easy it was to build your own fire pit.

"It's not any more difficult than arranging a few flowers in a vase," Granny said breathlessly as she hefted one of the large concrete blocks.

Granny was full of it, Dylan thought.

"We're both in our seventies," his mother said. "If she can do it, I can, too."

"More like seventy-nine and a half for you," he muttered.

His mother's eyes narrowed. "What did you say?"

Dylan searched his brain for a more diplomatic way to say what needed to be said, and then he spotted the elderly woman on the laptop screen dragging a forty-pound bag of ready-mix cement.

"You're nuts, if you think for once second I'm going to stand by and allow you to hurt yourself trying to haul concrete blocks and sacks of concrete mix bigger than you around the backyard."

"Allow me?" Virginia raised a brow. "I had a father, and his name wasn't Dylan. You don't tell me what I can or cannot do."

Exhaling, Dylan refilled his mug with coffee, wishing it were something stronger. "Nope. Can't tell you a thing." He swallowed the words *stubborn* and *hardheaded* with a sip of the black coffee. "It's why I picked up your order myself, and it's currently residing under my carport."

"B-but," Virginia sputtered, "you can't do that."

"Already done," Dylan confirmed.

"Well, you can just drive that pickup of yours around the corner and get my goods." She raised her mug to her lips.

"No can do, Mom."

She slammed the mug down on the table so hard Dylan thought it cracked. "You're being ridiculous."

"No, what's ridiculous is you thinking an eighty-year-old woman can do a job that's backbreaking work for a man half her age."

"I'm seventy-nine," she sniffed.

"Either way you cut it, too damn old to be laboring in the hot sun."

"Humph. Most folks thought forty-eight was *too damn old* for me to endure two days of labor pushing out a ten-pound baby with a head the size of a watermelon, but you're sitting here, aren't you?"

Dylan rolled his eyes toward the ceiling at the familiar refrain. An only child, he'd arrived years after his folks had given up on ever becoming parents. They were both young at heart, and their age hadn't been much of a factor when he was growing up.

However, Father Time was undefeated.

Two years ago, just as the elderly couple celebrated

his mother completing her final round of chemo for breast cancer, his father's heart gave out, at the age of eighty-one. Six months later, Dylan had moved back to Cooper's Place so he could look out for and spend as much time as he could with his remaining parent while he still had her.

It was a decision that cost him his hard-earned position as a homicide detective, and his marriage. So although he considered himself a reasonable man, when it came to anything that could affect his mother's well-being, he wouldn't budge.

Dylan noticed the cookie jar on the counter, reached inside and pulled out a cookie. With his penchant for sweets, it was usually the first thing he went for when he entered his mother's house. However, he'd been misled by the deceptive smell of those muffins.

He took a huge bite out of the homemade oatmeal-raisin cookie. He savored the flavors of genuine sugar and butter as he chewed.

"Don't try to playing the childbirth card, because it won't work. Not this time." Dylan opened his mouth to take a second bite.

"I'll take that." With reflexes of a teenager, Virginia bounded out of her chair and snatched the cookie from his hand. "Since you're in cahoots with that busybody Rosemary Moody, you can just go on down to the hardware store for homemade cookies."

"B-but, you can't do that." Dylan found himself stammering the same words his mother had said to him just moments before.

"Already done," she said, mimicking his deep voice. She leaned against the counter beside him and took a giant bite out of the confiscated cookie.

Dylan nudged her shoulder with his elbow. "Come on," he coaxed. "We both know Rosemary, or anybody else in this town, can't come close to your cooking."

It was no exaggeration. In addition to her countyfair blue ribbons, his mother had won the stove and other appliances now filling the kitchen as the first prize in a national bake-off. One of the perks of being back in his hometown was eating her cooking a few nights a week. She'd even occasionally brought dinner down to the police station on nights he'd worked late.

"I'm guessing you're the best cook in the state," he said.

Virginia snorted and then polished off the cookie in one last bite.

Dylan's stomach unleashed a rumble of protest. "Maybe even the entire country."

"Don't try playing the flattery card." His mother continued to flip the script by tossing his own words back in his face. Then she began to rattle off what she'd planned to cook for dinner. A menu that included buttermilk-fried chicken, macaroni and cheese, and honey-butter yeast rolls.

"That's some good eating, son." Virginia licked her lips. "Not to mention the lemonade layer cake I was considering whipping up for dessert."

She knew that cake was his favorite. It was the whole town's favorite. Last year she'd made two for a silent auction to raise funds for the town's library. They'd sold for over a hundred dollars each.

"So what time should I drop by for dinner?" Dylan ventured.

"Whenever." Virginia shrugged. "But your screwing with my fire-pit plans is making me lose my appetite. I think I'll just microwave a couple of frozen dinners. We can have fruit for dessert," she said. "How does a nice crisp apple sound to you?"

If there was a possibility of lemonade layer cake in his immediate future, an apple sounded about as appetizing as the muffin he'd sampled earlier.

"Look, Mom." Dylan's tone was conciliatory as he looked down at her. "I'd like to propose a compromise."

In the time he'd spent as his small town's police chief, employing the art of compromise had resolved most of the disputes that had cropped up. So different from Chicago, where they'd been settled with gun or knife violence before he'd been called to the scene.

"I'm listening," Virginia said, but her chin remained tilted at a stubborn angle.

"I'll drop by this evening. After we both enjoy your fabulous dinner and my favorite cake, I'll watch that episode of *Granny's Old House* and we'll make plans to build that fire pit together." With him doing all the heavy lifting, he thought, not saying that part aloud. "How does that sound to you?"

His mother sighed. "Okay, I guess."

Dylan leaned down and kissed his mother's wrinkled cheek. "Great. Afterward, we can watch the baseball game."

"Game?" His mother chuckled. "I don't see why you don't just haul that television you got me down to your place, too."

"Because it was your Mother's Day present." His gaze automatically flicked toward the family room, where the eighty-inch television sat.

"Guess the sports package you added was for me, too?" A smile warmed the corners of her mouth as she picked up a tea towel and swatted him on the arm.

Raising his arm to block the light blow, Dylan noted the time on his watch. "Uncle Roy should be about done at the doc's by now. I'm going to head over to city hall," he said. "So we're on for dinner, right?"

His mother nodded. "Although it seems to me with half the single women in town sniffing after you that you could do a damn sight better than hanging out with me on a Friday night. Folks are gonna think you're a mama's boy."

Dylan liked to keep life simple, and in his experience relationships meant complications and headaches. Besides, he couldn't care less what anyone thought. He was no mama's boy, but as long as Virginia Cooper drew breath he intended to remain in Cooper's Place being as good a son to her as she had been a mother to him.

His phone vibrated. Retrieving it from his shirt pocket, Dylan saw the dispatcher's number flash on the small screen. "What's up, Marjorie?"

Seconds later, he swiped his thumb across the screen to end the call and headed for the door.

"What's going on?" his mother called out to his retreating back.

"It's Wilson," Dylan said. "He's in the emergency room."

Chapter 5

Lola stared absently at her hand while the doctor rattled off a list of instructions. She barely heard a word, her thoughts bouncing between the injured officer she'd brought to the hospital's emergency room, and calculating how much driving time she'd have to make up once she got back on the road.

"The liquid adhesive should fall off in five to ten days. By that time your cut should have healed." The physician looked up at her. "Meanwhile, if you notice any redness, swelling, increased pain, or run a fever, seek additional medical attention."

Lola hadn't thought the small cut on the heel of her palm warranted medical attention in the first place. However, the scrub-clad woman behind the ER registration desk had seen the blood-soaked tissue clutched in Lola's hand, and had shuttled her into a treatment room opposite the one Officer Wilson had been whisked into.

A pale and unconscious Officer Wilson.

"About that cop I brought in..." Lola started, but the doctor wagged an admonishing finger and shook her head.

"I've already told you twice. I'm not at liberty to give out information on his condition," she said.

Lola tried again. "Please. All I want to know is if he's going to be okay."

Ignoring her plea, the physician pulled a pen from her lab coat and scribbled on a form attached to a clipboard. She looked over her shoulder at the nurse, who had returned to the room. "This patient is ready to be discharged."

The doctor left, and Lola hopped off the examination table. The liquid stitches sealing the cut on her hand had already begun to dry into a protective film. Still, she used her other hand to heft her bag onto her shoulder.

The nurse checked that she had understood the doctor's instructions, handed Lola a pen and pointed to a signature line on the clipboard. Lola caught a glimpse of the clock on the wall as she signed the form. She needed to get back on the road soon. However, she couldn't leave without confirming the cop would indeed be all right.

"I'm concerned about Officer Wilson. Can you tell me now how he's doing?" Lola hoped the nurse would be more forthcoming than her colleague.

The woman readjusted the stethoscope draped around her neck and then shook her head, just as the doctor had. "Sorry, but privacy laws won't allow it," she said. "But what I can do is check whether Officer Wilson's able to give his permission for me to update you, or maybe one of his family members who's here."

"I'd appreciate it," Lola said.

"I'll walk you out to the waiting area," she said, as they headed toward the door. "By the way, I'm Avis."

"Lola," she said automatically, and then remembered the nurse had seen her name on the hospital forms.

"I recognized you the moment you walked into our ER." The nurse nudged Lola's side with an elbow as they walked down the corridor, and lowered her voice to a conspiratorial whisper. "So, did you cut your hand beating up on Todd Wilson like you did that guy on the airplane?"

"What?" Lola asked, stunned.

Avis looked her up and down, shook her head and laughed. "You're a skinny thing, but those fists of yours must pack quite a punch when somebody gets on your bad side."

"B-but I didn't…"

"Don't bother denying it." The nurse waved a dismissive hand through the air. "I saw the video of that passenger you walloped on television again last night. It was the one of him being taken off the plane in a wheelchair, screaming in pain."

"Listen, that video doesn't tell the real story." Lola tried to explain.

The woman continued as if she hadn't heard a word. "Now, I'm not saying violence is the answer, but I have to admit to wanting to open a can of whup ass on Officer Wilson myself a few weeks ago."

Lola opened her mouth to try explaining again, and then promptly closed it. She didn't need to prove herself to a woman she'd just met in some hick town. Her goal was to arrive at that television studio on Monday morning looking fabulous. She needed to win over the viewership of *America Live!* and show her family all they'd lost by dumping her.

Just find out if that cop is okay, and get back on the road.

"Do you know what he did?" Avis's question broke into Lola's thoughts. The nurse didn't bother waiting for a response. "Well, my grandfather was downtown, and he bought himself a candy bar from the dollar store on account of his blood sugar, which can get a bit low at times. Anyway, he accidently dropped the wrapper on the sidewalk, and that Todd Wilson gave him a citation for littering. Littering, of all things!"

It sounded like littering to Lola, but she refrained from saying so.

"Gramps had hip replacement surgery, and still walks with a cane. If he had bent over to pick up that candy wrapper he wouldn't have been able to pick himself up off the street. Thank goodness our police chief is a reasonable man." Avis continued to talk without taking a breath. "Once I took Gramps to the police station and explained, the chief dismissed the ticket immediately."

Now in the hospital's waiting area, Lola cleared her throat to get the chatterbox nurse's attention. "You were going to try to get Officer Wilson's permission to update me," she reminded her. Then she looked down at her blood-and-dirt-encrusted clothes. "Also, where's the ladies' room? I'd like to clean up a bit and change my clothes."

"Oh, of course. There's a bathroom right near the emergency-room entrance," Avis said. "I'll see what I can find out and meet you back here."

Lola cleaned up as best she could in the public ladies' room and changed into a clean top and shorts she'd retrieved from her suitcase. She returned to the small waiting room, which was empty except for chairs lining the walls and a television. She rested her weighty purse in one of the hard plastic chairs and sat down beside it.

Sighing, she glanced up at the television. A commercial for a fast-food restaurant was on, and the image of the most mouthwatering hamburger Lola had ever seen filled the screen.

"Burger Tower," a voice-over announcer said. "Coming soon to Ohio."

Lola licked her lips and then looked around the small room for the remote control. She didn't want to be tempted by forbidden burgers, when all she had to look forward to later was a tasteless shake made from the protein mix in her purse.

Remote in hand, she aimed it at the television. She flipped through the channels but found nothing of interest.

Lola sighed at the screen. Hearing her phone ringtone, she turned to her purse. A sign near the television confirmed that using mobile phones was permissible in the waiting room, so she opened the mouth of her bag wide and gingerly stuck her hand inside.

The small phone rested near the top of the multitude of items she'd deemed necessities. Her talent agent's number lit up the small screen.

"Listen, honey," Jill said without preamble. "A friend of mine just tipped me off that some hidden-camera reality show is looking to pull one of their practical jokes on you. I think it's called—"

"Celebrity Pranks," Lola finished. *Tell me something I don't already know.* She thought about the cameraman and the guy in the clown costume she'd eluded back in Nashville, and stifled a grunt.

"Yeah, that's it," her agent said. "Word is they want to goad you into losing your temper. Tap into your notoriety, after that crap you pulled on the airplane, to boost their ratings."

"How many times do I have to tell you, I was trying to help an older gentleman—"

"Whatever you say," Jill interrupted.

Lola exhaled a long, weary breath. Explaining herself to people who refused to listen was getting old. In fact, she was fed up to her eyeballs with it.

"I just wanted to give you a heads-up, so you'll be on the lookout for anything suspect," Jill said. "We need you to show that *America Live!* audience there's more to you than what they've seen on social media and tabloid television. We don't want you on that practical jokes show looking like you could use a course in anger management."

"Don't worry. I'll be fine." Lola tossed the phone into her purse. As far as *Celebrity Pranks* was concerned, she was on high alert, and there was no way she was going to allow that show to make a jackass out of her.

Dylan wanted to be wrong, but he couldn't shake the feeling Todd Wilson wasn't being completely honest with him.

"I still don't understand how you went from issuing a speeding ticket to being knocked unconscious." He watched as the young officer sitting at the edge of the hospital gurney averted his gaze and then blinked rapidly. Gestures Dylan had learned back in the police academy were signals of a normally truthful person telling a lie.

"Heard the lady who brought him in is a real bruiser," Dr. Hadley chimed in. He dropped into a tray the instruments he'd used to stitch up the back of the young officer's head. "Our Wilson here got off easy. Word is she got mad a few days ago, went all MMA fighter on an airplane."

"Is that so?" Dylan asked absently, dismissing the doc's commentary as a tall tale built on gossip that had been embellished by too many mouths. If a woman had gone ballistic on a plane, he'd surely read it in the morning newspaper.

The doctor nodded and pulled off his latex gloves.

"I figure she got the jump on Wilson here when he tried to give her a speeding ticket. Knocked him to the pavement in one punch," he said. "In fact, my partner's treating the woman's hand. I think she's an actress or some kind of model…" Doc Hadley's voice faded. "I forget exactly what Avis said the woman did for a living."

Dylan remained focused on his officer, preferring to hear Wilson's account of how he'd ended up in the hospital's emergency room. "Tell me again what happened. Start from where you asked the motorist for her license and registration."

The young officer hesitated. "Uh…yeah, guess it was like the doc said. She came out of nowhere."

"*You guess* or you're sure?"

"Um, I guess… I mean, I'm sure."

Dylan disappointedly noted Wilson's eyes darted left, which meant there was a high probability he was accessing the creative side of his brain rather than his memory. However, Dylan didn't have to call upon his academy training or his experience as a homicide detective to know the officer's evasive responses to the questions were suspect.

He was about to press him on it when a hospital employee pushing a wheelchair entered the room. "Afternoon, Chief." He greeted Dylan first and then turned to the gray-haired physician. "They're ready for Wilson down in radiology, Doc."

Dr. Hadley addressed his patient. "I've ordered a CT scan and a few more tests. If they check out, you should be able to go home in a couple of hours."

Wilson avoided making eye contact with Dylan as he walked over and sat in the chair.

"I still have a few questions," Dylan said. Actually, he had a lot of questions for Officer Wilson and not many answers.

"Can they keep until later, Chief?" the doctor asked.

Dylan nodded, returning the pen and small notebook to the shirt pocket of his uniform. The odd interaction with the rookie officer continued to niggle at him as he walked out of the treatment room.

"Chief?"

Dylan turned around at the sound of his title, which he answered to more than his name nowadays. "Afternoon, Avis."

"The woman involved in the situation with Wilson is in the waiting area hoping to get an update on his condition," the nurse said. "Her name's Lola Gray."

Good, Dylan thought, as he walked down the hospital corridor toward the waiting area. Maybe she could tell him exactly what had happened out on Old Mill Road. He also had to admit to being curious to see a woman whose fists had earned her quite a reputation.

"Is that you, Chief?"

Dylan had been so busy speculating about the woman in the waiting room, he hadn't seen the overall-clad Jeb Dixon walking toward him. "Yeah, it's me," he said.

The farmer squinted behind the thick lenses of his glasses as if he were confirming it for himself.

"You and the wife doing all right?" Dylan asked.

Jeb didn't leave his farm often. Dylan figured either he or someone in his family must be ill if he was at the hospital in the middle of the afternoon.

"We're both good." The farmer took off his cap and scratched his head, then replaced it. "Actually, I came here looking for you. I stopped by the station, but Marjorie said you were here with young Wilson."

"What do you need?" Dylan asked.

"I had my daughter drive me to town because I witnessed a crime. Wanted to report it to you directly."

"What kind of crime?"

"At first I thought it was a kidnapping, but if Wilson is here, then maybe not."

"He's here," Dylan confirmed.

"Is the kid going to be okay?" Jeb asked. "He took quite a beating."

Dylan had seen the rookie cop just moments ago. He'd had a head injury, of course, and his uniform was dirty. However, his face was free of the bruises or scratches that would have indicated he'd been in a scuffle.

"The doc just took a look at him. He should be fine."

Jeb nodded. "Glad the woman at least had the decency to bring him here for help."

Dylan pulled the notebook and pen from his uniform pocket. So far, he'd heard more gossip than facts, and Wilson's accounting of events had been sketchy at best. An eyewitness could fill in the blanks for him. He took in the thick spectacles as he looked at Jeb.

At least he hoped.

"Tell me exactly what you saw."

"Well, I was in the fields on my tractor, checking on my sweet corn, when I saw a red car speeding like a bat out of hell on Old Mill Road, with the police car chasing it. I knew it was a police car on account of the blue lights were flashing." He paused and stroked the gray stubble on his chin. "Although at the time I didn't know if it was you or Wilson behind the wheel. But once he got out of the cruiser, I knew it wasn't you. A couple of linebackers would have had a time of it trying to take down a big guy like you." Jeb paused and looked up. "What are you—six-three, six-four?"

Dylan didn't answer. He let Jeb continue, waiting for him to eventually tell his version of the incident out on Old Mill Road.

"Anyway, a slip of a woman couldn't have knocked you out and then dragged you to her car like a sack of potatoes. I told my daughter so on the drive into town," the farmer said.

Dylan tapped his pen against his notepad. He needed to rein in Jeb's tangential nature and get to the bottom of this incident. "Did you actually see the motorist strike Officer Wilson?"

"Yes, sir. I believe I did."

"Did she hit him or not?" Dylan asked. His witness's answers sounded nearly as shifty as his officer's.

"One minute he was standing, and the next he was

on the ground with her standing over him," Jeb said. "You tell me."

Exhaling, Dylan tried again. "I wasn't there. Is it possible Wilson might have stumbled or fallen?"

The young officer could be clumsy at times, especially when he was nervous, so it was a possibility.

Jeb shook his head. "Nope, I'm pretty sure she decked him."

"But did you *see* her do it?" Dylan asked.

"I saw the whole thing with my own two eyes."

Dylan studied the thick lenses in Jeb's glasses and feared his witness's eyesight was as dependable as his answers. "How far away would you say you were from the road?"

The farmer shrugged. "Close enough to see it, but too far to get to them before the woman threw him in the car and took off."

"Was she facing him or did she attack him from behind? Did she hit him with her open hand or closed fist?"

Jeb shook his head and waved a dismissive hand at the more specific questions. "I don't know about all that, Chief," he said. "I just know what I saw."

And that didn't appear to be much, Dylan thought. "Thanks for coming into town to report it," he said aloud. "I'll give you a call if I have any more questions."

He'd gleaned precious little from interviews with Wilson and Jeb. Dylan looked at the few notes he'd taken. It was time he went to the source. He continued down the long corridor and turned the corner to the hospital's waiting room. He stopped short in the doorway.

The sight of long brown legs, crossed at the ankles and showcased by a pair of thigh-grazing shorts he was sure violated at least three town ordinances, grabbed his attention and held it.

Damn. His gaze unwittingly traveled the length of them. The journey from the tops of her firm thighs to the pink-painted toes peeking out of high-heeled sandals was like a Sunday drive—long, slow and easy. He took the trip twice.

She hadn't noticed him yet. A curtain of dark hair shielded the side of her face as she rummaged through a giant pink purse. Dylan's errant gaze slid to the curves of her calves and lingered.

The word *knockout* came to mind all right, but in an entirely different context than the way Doc and Jeb had used it.

Get a grip, man.

A Cooper's Place lawman was in the hospital, and this woman was suspected of putting him here. It wouldn't do to have the town's only other cop incapacitated, waylaid by legs that seem to go on for miles and *miles*. Legs that made him want to…

Dylan closed his eyes briefly, forcing back illicit images of the sexy legs before him and replacing them with the sight of Wilson just minutes ago being taken by wheelchair for tests. It was time Dylan stopped acting as if he'd never seen a hot pair of legs before, and did his job. Besides, a woman with her reputation for brawling more than likely had taken a few punches to the face and it probably showed.

Standing in the doorway, he cleared his throat to get her attention. "Lola Gray."

She looked up from the massive pink bag and tossed her dark hair over her shoulder. Dylan sucked in a breath as her movements revealed a face so exotically beautiful it kept him from stealing another peek at her legs.

Almond-shaped eyes and lips slicked with something pink and glossy dominated her perfectly symmetrical features, giving credence to at least one of the rumors churned out from the gossip mill. She had the looks to be a model or actress.

The woman in front of him was indeed a knockout. Again the word he'd already begun to associate with her popped into his head. So did another one: *trouble*. And Lola Gray looked like a ton of it.

Dylan flipped the switch to cop mode. Unlike his rookie officer, he'd had plenty of experience interviewing suspects and shielding his thoughts. There wasn't anything Ms. Gray could throw at him that he couldn't handle. He noted her small hands, including her fists.

"We need to have a talk," he said, entering the room.

The woman's eyes, fringed with thick lashes that appeared to touch her high cheekbones when she blinked, widened. Dylan caught a glint of temper in them before they narrowed.

"Don't you people ever give up?"

What the... Dylan was about to ask her what she was referring to when she looked around the room, muttering. He could make out the words *hidden cameras* and *clowns*, but the rest of what she said was unintelligible. Exhaling, he undid the top button on his uniform. He might as well get comfortable. It appeared this interview was going to be as frustrating as the ones he'd tried conducting with Wilson and Jeb.

Only this one could very well end with an arrest.

"Look, Ms. Gray," he said, walking toward the row of chairs where she was seated. "I need to talk to you," he repeated firmly, hoping she'd grasp the seriousness of the situation.

She rose from the chair and met him in the middle of the small room. A wicked smile spread over those glossy lips as she touched a finger to the brief expanse of bare chest revealed by the opened button.

"Oh, I'll just bet you do."

Chapter 6

Celebrity Pranks had overplayed their hand.

This man was too sexy to be a cop, Lola thought. His face was all hard planes and masculine angles, softened by dark chocolate eyes with thick lashes and lips that appeared soft and very kissable. Her gaze lingered on those lips before drifting to the day's worth of beard hugging his strong jawline, and then finally to the bangin' body that screamed *stripper* loud and clear.

But Lola wasn't falling for the ruse. Still, she had to give the show credit.

Good Lawd, they'd hired a fine one.

His body brought one of her late grandmother's sayings to mind: "Built like a brick house." Muscles strained against his supposed uniform, tempting Lola to finish what he'd started. Her hands itched to grab him by the collar, undo the rest of the buttons on his shirt and tear it right off his back.

She held off. Why risk breaking a fingernail? He'd come out of his clothes soon enough, seeing how it was his job.

And she could hardly wait.

"Well, *Officer*," she said, emphasizing his title.

"Actually, I'm the police chief here," he corrected. "Chief Dylan Cooper."

"Ooh, even better." Lola tapped her fingertip against his hard chest, before reluctantly pulling it away. "I'm dealing with a boss."

Frowning, he stared down at her, and Lola nearly laughed aloud at the confused expression on his face. Apparently, he was used to having an unsuspecting victim to pull a prank on, but the real joke was on him and the show. Despite the uniform, complete with a fake tin badge, Lola knew exactly who this man was and what he'd come here to do—and she was ready.

"Ma'am, I don't think you realize how much trouble you could potentially be in," he said.

The timbre of his deep voice sent a shiver down to her toes, which curled against the straps of her sandals. She'd bet *Chief Cooper* or whatever his real name was came home after a night of gyrating that body with women's handprints all over him and a G-string crammed with dollar bills.

Already she was having difficulty keeping her hands to herself. Lola figured she'd have to sit on them when he stripped down to nearly nothing.

She craned her neck to look up at him. At five foot ten inches tall, she towered over most men when she wore heels, but not this one.

"Mister, oh…" Lola briefly covered her mouth with her fingertips in a dramatic gesture she hoped conveyed to both him and whoever was monitoring the footage from the show's well-hidden camera that she knew they were full of it. "I mean Chief," she corrected. "Haven't you heard? Trouble is my middle name."

He shook his head, before lightly grasping her shoulders with his large hands. His deep brown eyes bored intently into her eyes as if he were examining them. "Are you high on something?" he asked, and then looked over her shoulder. "Are there drugs in your bag? Or on you?"

Lola threw her head back and laughed. These people were really pulling out all the stops. She dabbed at the tears in her eyes. Then an idea popped into her head. Maybe she should flip the script, she thought, and pull a prank of her own.

Don't do it, her sensible side warned, but it was overruled by an impulse too delicious to resist.

"Of course I'm not high. I don't do drugs," she said.

He dropped his hands to his sides, and Lola instantly missed their warmth penetrating her bare skin. She couldn't recall the last time she'd been touched by a man who wasn't just an assistant on a photo shoot positioning her for the camera.

Then Lola remembered. This man was also on a job. Moreover, she had a tremendous opportunity waiting for her that could turn into a dream career if she played her cards right. So she needed to wrap up things with *Chief Cooper*, check on the real cop she'd brought here unconscious earlier and hit the road.

"Look, this has been amusing, but I'm a busy woman." Lola looked at the clock on the wall and then back to him. "Just do what you came to do and get it over with."

His stone face was unreadable. Only an almost undetectable tic along the cop-slash-stripper's jawline revealed his annoyance that this scene wasn't unfolding the way he and *Celebrity Pranks* had planned.

"I've tried to do just that ever since I walked through the door." He pulled a pen and small pad from his shirt pocket. "Let's begin with what happened out on—"

Unable to believe the guy was still playing cop, Lola abruptly snatched the pen and pad from his hands. She flung them to the other side of the room.

"What the—" he began.

Lola folded her arms across her chest. "Either strip or, as the old saying goes, get off the pot."

"Huh? Strip? What on earth are you talking about?"

Her gaze fell below his belt, before returning to meet his. She lifted a brow and watched his jaw drop as he grasped her meaning. Lola figured the pranks weren't so hilarious when the celebrity they selected to play stooge had them all figured out.

This guy was good, Lola thought again. She'd nearly bought his surprised act. Maybe he was stripping while he waited on his break as an actor. He was certainly good-looking enough. He must drive the women at the club he worked at wild.

Lola had to admit to hotly anticipating the private show to come.

"Are you nuts?" he asked incredulously.

"Do you use this innocent bit in your act? I'll bet it, along with those chocolaty-brown eyes of yours, melts the panties right off 'em."

"Act? What act?"

Lola sighed. "I've just about reached the end of my patience waiting on you to take off that costume and shake that sexy ass of yours."

His dark eyes rounded. "Oh, my God," he whispered. "You actually believe I'm a…" His voice faded.

"Well, what are you waiting on?" Lola asked. "Or do I need to grab my wallet and start making it rain?"

The "Chief's" mouth opened and closed again, making him look like a fish gasping for air. "I can assure you I'm this town's police chief." His full lips firmed into a line.

"Yeah, yeah, yeah." Lola dismissed his declaration with a wave of her hand.

"Lady, I am not a stripper."

Fed up with the innocent act, Lola decided it was time to show him and the producers, once and for all, that they'd messed with the wrong woman. As her brother often said, the best defense is a good offense.

"What you need is a little loosening up to get this show on the road and that cop costume on the floor." She hoped wherever the hidden camera was stashed it captured the look on his face when she laid her next move on *Chief Cooper*.

Lola fisted his shirt collar and yanked the stunned stripper toward her, a move that left those lips of his scant inches from hers. She stared at them a moment, before licking her own.

Why the hell not, she thought. Who knows when she'd be this close to a man this gorgeous again? Besides, this was something best done before he got naked.

"Maybe this will get you in the mood." With the element of surprise tilted in her favor, Lola stood on the tips of her toes and closed the scant inches separating their lips.

His body stiffened in reaction to the bold move. His mouth, which had appeared so kissable moments ago, was as hard against hers as his broad chest. Lola shouldn't have felt disappointed. After all, they were strangers. The man was on a job, and her only intention had been to make it as difficult as possible.

She was on the verge of unfurling her fingers from his collar when his mouth suddenly softened and his big body relaxed. He ran his tongue over the seam of her lips and she parted them, now eager to see if he tasted as good as he looked.

He did.

Lola moaned as his tongue delved into her mouth. Kissing him had been her big brainstorm to throw the man off his game. However, it appeared the stripper name "Chief" suited him, because he'd taken control of both the kiss and the game.

Lola clutched his collar to keep from melting against him and sliding onto the floor. His tongue continued to explore her mouth in strokes as slow and easy as a summer afternoon. She felt his large hand at the base of her back, and unexpected warmth flowed through her.

He smelled of sunshine, and his embrace made her feel at home, as if she'd been waiting to kiss him her entire life. And she didn't want to stop. Apparently, the feeling was mutual. The hand at her back pulled her closer, and Lola wrapped her arms around his neck.

He felt, he smelled, he tasted so damn good, she thought, pressing against him.

Then she remembered.

This wasn't real. The man was working, and his job was to make a fool out of her.

Still, it took her traitorous body a moment to get on the same page as her brain. Releasing his collar, Lola planted her palms on his chest and pushed, wrenching her mouth away from his. A foot of space now separated them, but their gazes remained locked.

Lola steeled herself against the obviously practiced look of surprise on his face. It didn't matter how great a kisser he was or that he had a body that would play a starring role in her fantasies for nights to come. She wasn't about to give *Celebrity Pranks* the satisfaction or video footage of her looking as if she was falling for a stripper.

Time to take back the control she'd momentarily lost along with her damned mind. *Take this*, she thought.

She rounded the *police chief* and with her good hand smacked him soundly on the ass.

"Now take off your clothes and dance!"

The sound of female laughter drew Lola's attention to the doorway of the waiting room. The nurse she'd met earlier leaned against the doorjamb with her arms folded over her chest. "Now that's a sight I'd like to see myself." Avis winked. "I see you've gotten acquainted with our chief of police."

Lola's jaw dropped.

"P-police chief?" she croaked, hoping she'd heard the woman wrong.

"Yes, *police chief.*" The deep baritone of the man she'd assumed was a stripper rumbled behind her, confirming the fact that she'd really screwed up this time.

Lola closed her eyes briefly. She covered her mouth, which still tingled from the aftershocks of his kiss. One thought reverberated through her head.

Oh, crap.

"Do you finally have it through your head that I'm not an *entertainer*?" Dylan asked. He didn't wait for an answer before firing off another question. "What made you think something so absurd in the first place?"

He watched her slowly remove her hand from her mouth to reveal the lips he'd tried to devour just moments ago. Her lipstick had been kissed away, leaving her lips a natural shade of pink he found even more enticing.

Fortunately, she'd put a stop to it, before a kiss that shouldn't have happened in the first place got totally out of hand. Otherwise, Avis might have walked in on an entirely different scenario, Lola Gray sandwiched between him and the wall, those long legs of hers wrapped around his waist.

Dylan drew an unsteady breath. Her out-of-the-blue kiss didn't disturb him as much as his reaction to it. What was the matter with him? This wasn't like him at all. He always kept his cool, especially when he was working. But one touch of this woman's lips had unleashed something inside him he hadn't known existed.

A need to get laid, he reasoned. It was the only explanation he could come up with for his uncharacteristic behavior.

It was just a kiss, but he was acting like a high school geek who'd garnered the attention of the homecoming queen. Dylan could feel Lola Gray as if she were still in his arms. The scent of her sultry perfume, exotic and spiked with coconut, clung to his uniform. Her sweet taste lingered on this tongue.

"Does this mean you won't be dancing naked, Chief?" the nurse asked from the doorway.

"No," Dylan said, emphatically. His eyes remained on Lola.

"That's too bad," Avis replied.

Dylan turned to the nurse and frowned. "I'm trying to conduct an investigation here, Avis. Do you mind?"

The nurse pulled away from the doorjamb. Her

eyes twinkled with amusement. "Okay, I'll go, but remember, the doc and I are just down the corridor if that spanking she was giving you gets out of hand."

"But I wasn't…" Lola Gray called out after Avis. It appeared as if she had more to say, but she sighed instead. She turned her attention back to him. "I apologize for the misunderstanding, Chief Cooper."

She launched into an explanation involving stalker reality shows and clowns that sounded just convoluted enough to be true. Dylan held up a hand to stop her.

"Let's just forget it, Ms. Gray," he said.

"I'd like that." She smiled up at him. Different from the wicked grin she'd bestowed upon him earlier, this smile beguiled him with its openness and warmth. "Oh, and about that…um, swat to your, uh, backside."

"Already forgotten." As he uttered the words, Dylan wondered if his own body language gave away the fact he wasn't being totally honest. He had a feeling it would be a long time before he would be able to put kissing her out of his head.

"So, did you come to update me on Officer Wilson's condition?" she asked. "He was still unconscious when I brought him here. I've been so worried. I couldn't leave until I knew for sure he would be okay."

"He's awake. The doc stitched up the back of his head and wants him to hang around for some tests before they boot him out of here. But it looks like he's going to be just fine."

"Great." She rested her hand on her chest and exhaled. "Now I can get back on the road."

Dylan had seen two sides to Lola Gray in the short minutes since they met. One was over the top and sexy as hell, the other conscientious and appearing genuinely concerned about Wilson's welfare. Neither suggested to him she was capable of assaulting the rookie officer.

"Not just yet," Dylan said. "I need to hear your version of what happened out on Old Mill Road."

"My version?" She raised a quizzical brow.

Dylan picked up the pen and pad she'd thrown across the room earlier, and then gestured toward the chairs. "Let's have a seat."

She eyed the clock on the wall. "Okay, but I don't have a lot of time."

Dylan sat down in a chair beside her. "You can start with how you ended up on Old Mill Road. It's off the beaten path. Not many people travel on it nowadays."

"There was an accident tying up traffic on the main road, and my GPS suggested a detour to avoid it," she said.

Wilson had radioed in to Dispatch that he'd pulled over a red Mustang, but the rest of what he'd said had been garbled by static. Dylan had spotted the car parked in front of the emergency room earlier and called in the Tennessee license plate. Marjorie reported back that the vehicle was indeed registered to Lola Gray, and it hadn't been involved in any illegal activity.

"Why did Officer Wilson pull you over?"

Dylan watched her as he waited for an answer to the question.

"Like you said, that road was pretty isolated." She shrugged, but unlike his officer, the woman looked him straight in the eye. "I couldn't resist the temptation of a fast car and the open road. So my foot got a bit heavy on the accelerator. Next thing I knew, blue lights were flashing in my rearview mirror."

Dylan listened as she continued to explain. Her version of events differed from both the victim's and the eyewitness's. She seemed more sure of herself than Wilson, but Dylan had to take into consideration the rookie had a minor head injury. Also, despite his eyesight, Jeb seemed just as certain of her attacking Wilson.

Dylan had known both Wilson and Jeb a lot longer than he'd known Lola Gray, but his gut instinct told him hers was the most accurate account of the incident.

A gut instinct that may have been compromised by a sweet mouth and a pretty smile.

"When I couldn't summon help by phone or using Officer Wilson's radio, I dragged him to my car and brought him straight to the hospital," she concluded.

"So at no time did you strike Officer Wilson?"

She scrunched up her face. "What? Of course not. What gave you that idea?" Her confused expression morphed into a scowl. "Oh, I get it now. You saw one of those stupid tabloid news reports. Now you believe

I'm a Neanderthal that goes around beating up people whenever the mood strikes me."

Dylan looked pointedly at the tiny cut on her hand. The doc had speculated she'd injured it coldcocking Wilson. However, Doc Hadley hadn't been the one to actually treat what appeared to be a minor injury.

"I already told you. I cut my hand on a pair of scissors in my bag," Lola Gray said.

Scissors seemed like an unusual item to keep in a handbag, Dylan thought. Then again, the thing looked more like a carry-on suitcase than a purse.

She rolled her eyes and heaved what sounded like an exasperated sigh. Grabbing the bag from the chair on the other side of her, she plopped it on her lap. She opened a side pocket.

"I put them in a separate compartment so I wouldn't cut myself on them again," she said.

Sure enough, there was a pair of scissors with what Dylan recognized as dried blood on them. She started to reach for them, but he stopped her.

"Don't touch them," he cautioned. "They're evidence."

"Evidence? In what?"

"The possible assault of Officer Wilson."

"Assault? What assault?" Big brown eyes blinked up at him as realization dawned. Her expression made him feel as if he'd just snatched a bucket of candy from a child trick-or-treating. "You think I... B-but I explained what happened. He took one look at my bloody hand and passed out. The only time I touched him was to try to help."

"Officer Wilson says different. He claims you took him by surprise and knocked him out," Dylan said.

"He's mistaken," she countered. "He hit his head hard. It must have left him confused."

"There's also an eyewitness to the incident," Dylan began.

"Who? I didn't see anyone," Lola said. "And if they claim to have seen everything, why didn't they help?"

"He says he was too far away to get to you, but saw Officer Wilson stop your car."

"Good," she said. "Then they should be able to confirm what I told you."

Dylan shook his head. "The witness's account substantiates Officer Wilson's allegation against you."

"He's wrong. They're both wrong. Sure, I'm guilty of speeding, but that's it." Lola clamped a hand on Dylan's arm. "You've got to believe me."

The thing was, he did believe her. *Or, deep down, did he just want to believe her?* Regardless, he had a job to do.

"Do you think I would have brought him here or stuck around to see how he was doing if I had hurt him?" she asked.

Dylan removed her hand from his arm and stood. "I think it would be best if we continued this conversation at the police station."

"Police station? But why?" She asked another question before he could answer. "Am I under arrest?"

"No, but I'm detaining you until I know what really happened out on Old Mill Road."

Chapter 7

"I don't have time for this."

Lola repeated the words for what felt like the hundredth time. She stole a glance at the police chief's strong profile as he drove the black pickup from the hospital along the small town's bustling main thoroughfare.

Mirrored aviator sunglasses shielded his eyes against the late-afternoon sun, and the rest of his deep brown face was set as if it had been carved on the side of a mountain. Lola would have assumed he was as cold as stone, if she didn't know better. There was a blazing hot side to this man, and she'd nearly unleashed it.

Who knows where they'd be if she hadn't broken off that kiss and pushed him away?

Deep down she already knew the answer. They would have found a more private location, where they both would have done some stripping, and by the looks of him, she'd be experiencing her second orgasm about now.

Instead, she was on her way to jail.

"But you don't understand. I have a big job waiting on me in New York." Lola tried again to get through to him.

"So you've told me." He slowed in front of a small, one-story brick building that looked decades past its prime. Cooper's Place Public Safety Department was etched into stone above the entrance. A blue police department emblem emblazoned one of the glass double doors, and a red volunteer fire department emblem was on the other. Lola spied a fire truck parked in a bay at the opposite end of the building.

"It's an opportunity of a lifetime," she continued.

Parking in the space designated for the chief of police, he rounded the truck and opened the door for her.

"You told me that, too." His deep voice was robotic, devoid of emotion or any concern for her predicament. Apparently, he'd had no problem forgetting about their misguided kiss and had snapped immediately into cop mode.

It was time she wiped it from her mind, as well, and put an end to this small town farce before she got in any deeper. Ignoring the hand he held out to her, Lola remained rooted to the passenger's seat.

"I didn't do anything." She crossed her arms over her chest. "And I'm not letting you lock me up."

Lola uncrossed her arms. She clutched the pickup's armrest with her fingertips and braced herself to be hauled bodily from the truck. Instead, he rested a hand on top of the side door and removed his shades with the other. He glared at her a moment and then exhaled.

"Look, Ms. Gray, for what it's worth, I'm inclined to believe the incident went down exactly the way you say it did, and as the chief here, I'm able to exercise some discretion. It's why I'm only detaining you, instead of placing you under arrest," he said. "I need more time to get to the truth."

Lola relaxed her death grip on the armrest, but didn't let go.

"However, if you insist on making my job difficult, I *will* arrest you. Then I'll send for a sheriff's deputy to pick you up and transport you to the county jail so fast it'll make that pretty head of yours spin."

"Hold on." Lola blinked. "You believe me?"

Surprise stole the edge from his threat. Lately, it seemed she was constantly explaining herself, only to get a skeptical side-eye for her efforts. Not even her family believed her side of the story. She never expected the benefit of the doubt from someone she'd just met.

"At this point, yes, I do." His face was still impassive, but Dylan Cooper's deep brown eyes brimmed with a sincerity she didn't see often. Lola couldn't help feeling a twinge of disappointment when he covered them with his sunglasses. "So what's it going to be, wait here while I investigate or a holding pen at the county jail?"

He held out his hand, and she stared at it.

"Trust me," he said.

Finally, Lola put her injured hand in his, grabbed her oversize bag with the other and allowed him to help her down to the sidewalk. It was foolish to trust a man she barely knew, based on one kiss. Then again, the kiss wasn't the real reason Lola walked through the glass door with the police emblem he held open for her.

He believed her.

Still, common sense dictated she also needed to contact an attorney, ASAP. "Do I get to make my one phone call?"

He removed the sunglasses and stuck them in his shirt pocket. "Again, you're not under arrest. You can make as many calls as you wish."

He yanked open a second door to a large office space brimming with people and the buzz of conversations. It fell silent when they stepped inside. Every jaw dropped, and Lola could feel every eyeball in the room trained on her.

"What the...?" The cop beside her swore softly.

Before he could finish his question, a woman wearing workout clothes, with a baby perched on her hip, called out one of her own. "Is this the gal who beat the tar out of Wilson, Chief?"

Lola rolled her eyes toward the fluorescent lights attached to the ceiling. "I never touched him," she said.

The din of chatter, which had returned with a vengeance, drowned out her denial.

Another woman, this one in a red-striped waitress uniform with a nametag that read Tammy shouted out her two cents' worth. "Jeb popped by the diner. He says she was kicking ass and taking names out on Old Mill Road." Tammy jerked a thumb in Lola's direction. "Another one of my customers claims there's a video on the internet of her taking on a planeload of passengers single-handed."

A balding man, with what remained of his silver hair swept back into a ponytail, stepped forward, and Lola immediately noticed he'd also made the unfortunate fashion choice of pairing his knee-length khaki shorts with white athletic socks and sandals.

He examined her and then shook his head. "No way, Tammy." He crossed his arms over his ample chest, revealing a faded tattoo that read Born to Raise Hell on his forearm. "She's tall enough. I'll give you that, but she's too pretty to go around picking fights and too scrawny to win 'em."

The room erupted in laughter, accompanied by a few murmurs of agreement.

"Hold on a second." The former hell-raiser unfolded his arms and fished a pair of glasses from the pocket of his Hawaiian shirt. Squinting through the lenses, he continued to stare at her, and Lola doubted he'd raised much hell over the last decade or so.

"I know that face." His own wrinkled face brightened as recognition dawned. "I saw it in one of my wife's magazines. You're the lady in the ads for those vitamins for creaky joints."

Lola automatically issued another denial that was about as effective as the first one concerning Officer Wilson.

"No, Gary. That's not her." A rotund woman in a floral dress sidled up to the man. She wore a shade of orange lipstick Lola instantly identified as Espresso's Calypso Coral, and the matching peach blush staining her light brown cheeks was also their brand.

Finally, Lola thought. There was at least one person here who had a clue about her. It shouldn't have mattered so much in a room full of strangers. However, these false rumors about her, both in this town and nationwide, had taken on a life of their own.

The situation was getting out of hand.

Exhaling, Lola smiled at the woman Gary had called Rosemary, who was wearing products from the cosmetic line founded by Lola's late mother. The woman returned her smile with a toothy grin of her own.

"This here is a lady from the denture adhesive commercial," Rosemary said.

Lola's smile vanished, replaced by a frown. It didn't stop the woman from peeling back her coral-lipstick-covered top lip and tapping her teeth with a fingertip.

"See? It holds my partial in place all day, just like you said it would." She whipped out a cell phone from the pocket of her dress. "How about taking one of those selfies with me, so I can show it off at the garden club? Virginia Cooper took a picture with that hunky host of *Jeopardy* when he stayed at her B and B last year, but I'll bet none of them have a photo with the denture lady."

Lola groaned. This was exactly why she had to get out of this mess and haul tail to New York City, she thought, silently pleading with the woman to close her mouth and take those faux choppers off display. A gig hosting *America Live!* wouldn't just show her family they'd made a huge mistake in firing her, it would also help rid her of the senior citizen reputation both she and Espresso were desperate to shed.

"Enough!" A deep baritone rumbled over the din of conversations, silencing the room again and shaking the floor beneath Lola's feet. She'd been so caught up in the impromptu welcoming committee greeting, she'd forgotten Dylan Cooper was standing beside her.

She could feel the annoyance radiating off his big body. However, his face remained unreadable, except for that almost undetectable tic along his jawline.

He lifted his chin and peered over the heads of everyone as if he were looking for someone specific. "Marjorie," he called out.

"Is that you, Chief?" a muffled female voice buried in the crowd asked in reply.

The sea of people automatically parted. Guiding Lola by the elbow, the police chief walked her to the back of the large office, where a woman in a uniform was busy straightening what looked like both a jail cell and filing room. A telephone headset was clamped on her head. She pulled a pink satin pillowcase from the top of a tall filing cabinet and stuffed it with a lumpy pillow. She fluffed the pillow and then placed it on a pink-duvet-covered cot attached to the wall.

"What in the heck are you doing?" Dylan asked. "And what is half the town doing here?"

"I'm just straightening the place up a bit for company." The Miss Clairol redhead answered his question courteously, but her gaze remained trained on Lola. "Can't have our lone jail cell looking like a storage room when we're about to have a celebrity occupying it." She leaned in and lowered her voice to a hushed whisper. "I sent my sister over to Wal-Mart to pick up this bedding because I read both in the *National Enquirer* and *Vogue* that pink was your favorite color and that you only slept on satin sheets. By the way, I'm Marjorie. I'm the police and fire departments' dispatcher."

Marjorie looked at her expectantly, like an overly eager puppy awaiting a pat on the head, and Lola couldn't bear hurting the feelings of someone who'd gone through so much trouble for her.

"It's very…" She searched her brain for the right word.

"Ms. Gray isn't under arrest," the police chief said firmly. "Even if she was, inmates in our custody are not *company*."

Marjorie's face fell. "But everybody says she assaulted Wilson."

Lola opened her mouth to set the record straight,

again, but the chief stopped her with a single shake of his head, conveying a silent message for her not to bother. He turned to the dispatcher.

"You still haven't told me what all these people are doing here."

"They all heard there was a celebrity in town and wanted to get a look at her," Marjorie said. "Ms. Gray is the most excitement we've had in Cooper's Place in a long time."

"Yeah, she's been on TV and everything," someone from the crowd behind them yelled, and a chorus of voices rang out in agreement.

The chief faced the horde of people. "Everyone not here for official police business, please leave."

"Come on, Chief Cooper. You, of all people, shouldn't blame us for being a little starstruck," a man wearing a wifebeater and a tool belt wrapped around his thick waist said. "According to Avis over at the hospital, she walked in on you about to dance for the lady here, buck naked."

"Now that's a sight I'd like to see." The woman in the floral dress winked.

"Everybody. Out. Now." Dylan Cooper's words erupted from his in mouth in a menacing growl that promptly dispersed the impromptu gathering.

"So how did you get him to dance naked?" Marjorie lifted a brow. "Threaten to beat him up, too?"

Lola closed her eyes briefly, sucked in a deep breath and blew it out. This was just great, she thought. Not only was she wasting hours of driving time, she was being made out to be the town bruiser here. "I haven't threatened or assaulted anyone. All I did was drive my car too fast," she said, weary of issuing the same denial.

The dispatcher shifted her gaze to her boss. "So did you really dance—"

"Don't be ridiculous." He cut her off before she could finish the question. "Now, Ms. Gray has to make a phone call, and I have to make a few calls myself to try and make some headway into getting to the bottom of what happened to Wilson."

"Oh, your uncle's secretary has called a few times. He phoned himself the last time. Apparently, you've missed a meeting at city hall," Marjorie said. "I tried telling him you were busy with a case, but you know Roy."

Unfortunately, he did. "I'll take care of it." Dylan added it to the list of calls he needed to make, including one to the hospital. He wanted to know the moment Wilson was done with their tests.

Lola followed him to a desk on the other side of the room. "Make whatever calls you need," he said, then inclined his head toward an alcove. "Vending machines are over there. Bathroom is around the corner."

After pulling her phone and its charger from her bag, she dropped the heavy tote on the desk and collapsed into the office chair. She spied a side entrance to the building, and her impulsive side reared its head. "You seem pretty sure I won't make a run for it," she said.

The corner of his mouth, which Lola now knew firsthand tasted even better than it looked, quirked upward. "Just confident I'll catch you before you're halfway to that door." He snorted. "Then I'd have to lock you up in that pink palace Marjorie's fixing up special."

He glanced pointedly at the jail cell and then at her. "Your call?"

"I'll stick with the desk."

"Good choice." He looked at her bag. "I'm going to have to get those scissors so I can send them to the lab in Columbus."

"It's my blood. How long will it take to prove it?" Lola gnawed at her lip.

"I'll send them out today and should have a report sometime next week."

"But I can't hang around here that long."

"If I can uncover the truth quickly and your story holds up, you shouldn't have to. Regardless, I have to go by the book. I'll give this back to you in a few minutes." He picked up her bag from the desk. "Geez, what's in here?"

"Everything," Lola said.

"If I didn't know better, I'd think it was a pink body bag," he muttered as he walked over to a desk a few feet away from where she was seated.

Lola plugged the charger into the wall socket near the desk and stared at the green light on the charging phone. The police chief seemed sincere, and he could certainly kiss.

She glanced at the jail cell, where the dispatcher was busy replacing an old lampshade with a new pink one. Lola exhaled. As much as she dreaded reaching out to her family after the stunt they'd pulled, she was dangerously close to doing a stint in the pokey.

Lola swiped the phone's screen with her finger. She needed legal advice from her brother-in-law. Hopefully, her sister, who Lola was still annoyed with for treating her like the world's biggest screwup, would be busy behind her desk at Espresso's flagship Sanctuary Spa.

"Lola? Is everything okay?" Ethan asked without preamble.

"Is that my sister?"

Lola heard Tia's question, and her stomach dropped. "Ethan, please don't tell her it's—"

Too late.

After some muffled voices and a fumbling noise, her sister was on the line.

"What's wrong now, Lola?" Tia's question was more of a statement, as if the fact there was trouble was a foregone conclusion.

She was right, Lola thought grudgingly. Still, her sister's assumption was akin to Tia bouncing on her last nerve as if it was a backyard trampoline.

"Does there have to be something wrong for someone to have a conversation with their brother-in-law?" Lola asked.

Her big sister had a chill vibe and regularly exhorted the virtues of yoga and her special brew of calming tea—except when it came to Lola.

"In your case, yes," Tia said, emphatically. "And I'll bet the only reason you're calling Ethan is because he's a lawyer." She expelled a drawn-out sigh. "So what kind of chaos have you caused this time?"

Lola opened her mouth to once again dispute the accusation, but decided to save her breath. No one believed her these days, anyway.

Dylan Cooper believed you.

Lola's gaze automatically sought the police chief at his desk, talking on the phone. Goose bumps erupted on her bare arms at the memory of the scant moments she'd spent in his embrace. Too bad he wasn't a stripper. As good as he looked in that uniform, she wouldn't mind seeing him out of it. *Not at all.*

"You might as well spill it, because Ethan will tell me everything." Tia's voice threw a bucket of ice water on the heated images Lola's imagination had gotten carried away conjuring up.

"What about attorney-client privilege?" Lola countered.

Tia answered her with a harrumph. "I just put his phone on Speaker, so you can fill us both in on your latest calamity, and then we can figure out how to fix it for you."

This was indeed a calamity, Lola thought. However, her sister sounded so smug. Tia's tone, combined with the role she'd played in helping Cole railroad her in the Espresso boardroom, made her one of the last people Lola wanted to turn to for help. She'd fix her own mess.

"Never mind," Lola said.

"You had to have called for a reason," Tia pressed.

Lola made up a bogus explanation for the call and

ended it as quickly as she could. Deep down, she knew her sister loved her, and her brother did, too. However, the one thing Lola didn't have from them was the one thing she wanted more than anything: their respect.

She stared down at the phone in her hand. She'd fix this mess on her own.

She had to.

"Your phone calls go okay?"

Lola looked up to see the police chief placing her purse on the desk. "Yes and no," she said.

The expression on his handsome face was a mixture of confusion and what appeared to be genuine concern.

"Let's just say I was told what I needed to hear," she elaborated.

He nodded. "I'm headed out to Old Mill Road. It's getting late, and I want to take a look around before sunset," he said. "If you need anything, just let Marjorie know."

Lola stood abruptly as he turned to leave. "Wait!" She hefted her purse strap onto her shoulder. "You just can't leave me here. I'm coming with you."

"No, you're staying put. This is police business."

"But you need me to show you where it happened."

He shook his head. "I don't. The police cruiser is still at the scene," he said. "Besides, this is an investigation and right now you're the prime suspect."

Lola rested a hand on his forearm. She was the one whose future was at stake, and she wasn't putting her fate in someone else's hands. "You said you believed me, and that being chief gave you some leeway."

"True on both counts. Still, I'm not taking you with me to Old Mill Road."

"Why?" She raised a brow. "Scared if we're alone out there, I'll beat you up, too?"

A frown tightened his mouth, but didn't quite reach his hypnotic brown eyes. "Jokes like that are a bad idea for someone in your position."

"Maybe." Lola shrugged. "But since I seem to be stuck with the name, I might as well play the game."

Chapter 8

"So what's our plan for cracking the case, Chief?"

Dylan glanced at the woman in his pickup's passenger seat as he pulled out of his parking space, headed in the direction of Old Mill Road.

"*We* are not cracking anything," he reiterated. "And under no circumstances are you to interfere with this investigation."

"Of course not," she said.

"I'm serious, Ms. Gray. I only brought you along so your presence wouldn't cause more of a ruckus in town."

It wasn't his only rationale. Back in Chicago, Dylan had seen enough suspects reach out to family or a friend to know when it hadn't gone well. She'd shaken it off quickly, but not before the forlorn look on her face when she'd ended her phone call penetrated his thick skin.

His uncharacteristic reaction was all the more reason to get to the truth, and then he could either send her on her way or to the county jail.

"I don't know about you, but it feels silly to continue using surnames after the way we were all over each other at the hospital earlier."

Her statement threw him—right back to the feel of her in his arms, the taste of her mouth, and the sultry scent of her coconut-laced perfume filling his nostrils. Dylan shook away the illicit images racing through his head before they could get a grip.

"It's called keeping a professional distance." He stared through the truck's windshield as he drove slowly down Main Street, adhering to the twenty mile per hour speed limit. "Besides, I thought we'd agreed to forget it."

"I tried, but I can't seem to get it out of my head. Can *you*?"

Again, she'd tossed out something that knocked him off-kilter. Dylan found her stark honesty both bold and refreshing. It compelled him, despite his better judgment, to be just as honest.

"No, Lola. I can't forget kissing you, either," he said softly, enjoying the melodious feel of her first name rolling off his lips. He deepened his voice an octave, so his tone was firm. "However, it won't keep me from doing my job."

She shifted and then leaned back on the truck's leather seat. Out the corner of his eye, he saw she'd laid her head on the headrest. He could feel her eyes on him.

"Don't worry. I'm not angling to be the next Mrs. Cooper."

Her laugh elicited a chuckle from him.

"Good to know. I didn't make the last one very happy."

She raised her head. He turned briefly and caught her surprised expression. "I find that hard to believe."

"How come?" Dylan glanced at the time, illuminated on the dashboard. "We've known each other for what, an hour or two? For all you know, I could have been a horrible husband and made her life hell."

His eyes returned to the road as he continued to navigate through town, but again he could feel hers on him. Her heated gaze skimmed his chest and the bare arms revealed by the short sleeves of his summer uniform.

"Perhaps," Lola said. "But by the looks of you, I'm guessing she found some aspects of it deliriously satisfying."

Dylan heard her voice as she continued to talk, but the rest of what she said faded into white noise. His mind dropped him into the middle of a fantasy of kissing her again, naked in the backyard pool he'd had installed last summer, but rarely found the time to use. He imagined those long limbs of hers wrapped around his waist. Or perhaps on his shoulders, while he showed her just how deliriously satisfied he could—

"Well?" His passenger's question abruptly snatched him out of his fantasy and returned him to reality.

Dylan cleared his throat, hoping that would get his errant thoughts back on track. "Sorry, can you repeat the question?"

"I was asking how many hours a day you put in at the gym to maintain that body?"

"Enough to keep the Henderson brothers from kicking my behind."

"Henderson brothers?" Lola asked.

"Never mind them," Dylan said. "I have a question for you."

"Ask away."

"Do you always say exactly what's on your mind?"

Her long sigh filled the truck's interior. "Unfortunately, I do," she said. "I try hard to curb it, but usually what comes up, comes out—as in right out of my mouth."

"And you believe that's a bad thing?" Dylan stole a peek at her, before returning his gaze to the rich green farmland on the edge of Cooper's Place city limits. She'd been staring out the passenger's-side window, so he didn't see her face.

"Sure." She shrugged. "So does everyone else in my life, it seems."

"Actually, I find it refreshing."

"Really?" She laughed. "Then you're certainly in the minority."

From the little he knew of her, one of the things Dylan couldn't help liking about Lola Gray was her what-you-see-is-what-you-get nature. "I think you're fine as is. You shouldn't have to curb or change who you are for anyone," he said.

Silence followed his statement. The stretch of quiet echoed inside the truck. Dylan wondered what was on her mind as he slowed the truck to a halt at a stop sign, and then made a left turn onto Old Mill Road.

"That's the nicest thing anybody has said to me in a long time, Dylan Cooper," she said finally.

Something about her words tugged at his insides. With her looks, he assumed she was drowning in compliments. The woman was sexy, charming, easy to talk to, and in the short hours since he'd met her, Dylan found himself thinking of a better use for his king-size bed than falling asleep in it after a long day.

Get a grip, man!

Dylan gave himself a mental reprimand as he white-knuckled the steering wheel. He barely knew her, yet already he'd imagined making love to Lola Gray in his pool and in his bed.

For goodness sake, the woman was the prime suspect in the alleged assault on a police officer. Even though Dylan's gut told him she didn't do it.

Gut instinct had kept him alive back in Chicago. Now his gut was telling him to do his job, which regardless of how it turned out would get Lola out of Cooper's Place and his head.

"I couldn't help noticing everyone in town thinks they recognize you. So who are you, the creaky joint and denture adhesive lady, or the airplane version of Floyd Mayweather Jr.?" Dylan asked. He hoped segueing to a benign topic would keep inappropriate thoughts of the woman at bay, and the torture of seeing her incredible legs in shorts so miniscule they should be criminal.

Lola's laugh filled his ears. Despite the trouble looming over her head and a job she needed to get to, her laugh came free and easy. The more he heard it, the more Dylan liked it.

"Are you asking out of curiosity or as the police chief?" she asked.

"A little of both." He looked at her briefly and saw her eyes widen. "Why was my question so surprising?"

She squirmed in her seat, shifting her body toward him. "Everyone just assumes, they never ask me. And you've seen what happens when I try to explain." She shrugged. "It seems folks are happier with rumors and gossip."

"I'm not big on either. I'd rather hear it from your mouth," Dylan said.

"Actually, I'm a model, and until I was fired this morning, I was the face of Espresso Cosmetics," she said.

"The name sounds familiar. I think that's my mother's brand." He had a vague recollection of being dragged to their counters as a kid during occasional trips to the mall.

"Then your mom must be at least sixty," Lola said.

"Closer to eighty," Dylan confided.

He heard Lola sigh.

"That's one of our problems."

Dylan listened as she told him about the company's

stigma as makeup for women of a certain age, and how, despite her being in her twenties, people associated her with it.

"I can't help noticing you use the word *our* when you talk about Espresso Cosmetics, despite your being let go from your job with them. Is it out of habit?"

"No. They can't get rid of me that easily." She must have caught his confused expression, because she went on to explain. "Espresso was founded by my late mother, so I was actually fired from a company I partially own."

"How'd that happen?"

"There was the incident on an airplane... Well, I've actually found myself in the midst of quite a few messes. They weren't exactly my fault, but my brother, sister, their spouses and my father see it differently."

"Would this be the same airline incident that has the practical-joke television show you mentioned earlier following you, and half the town believing you're a woman who punches first and asks questions later?"

Lola nodded. "I can't believe you haven't seen the videos of me surrounded by airport security, or the passenger I supposedly beat so badly he needed a wheelchair. The darn things have been all over social media and television."

"Like I said, I'm not much into rumors or gossip," he said. "So I'll just ask you straight out, did you?"

"I didn't beat him up, but..."

Again, Dylan listened as Lola gave him a rundown of the incident. He didn't blame her for shoving the rude passenger's feet off the older man's head. In her place, he might have done the same thing or worse. However, he wasn't a woman or an elderly man, and because of his size, Dylan rarely had to repeat a request.

"Considering the situation, I admire you for stepping in and helping when no one else would. I also think you showed an incredible amount of restraint in dealing with that jerk," Dylan said finally. Just as she'd stepped up and gotten Wilson to the hospital. "You deserved a round of applause."

Lola giggled. "The passengers who weren't busy taking photos and filming me with their cell phones did clap."

They continued the ride in silence. Dylan lowered his speed when he spotted the police cruiser Wilson had been driving ahead.

Dylan felt a nudge at his biceps and glanced at the woman in the passenger's seat.

"I'm still trying to wrap my head around you not only believing me, but understanding how I got into the whole airline fiasco. You don't even know me, but you took my word as fact," she said. "Is it because of that kiss?"

Dylan parked his truck in front of the abandoned cruiser, and then shifted in his seat until he was facing her. He was a man of few words, who usually kept his thoughts to himself. However, for a second time, her openness prompted him to be just as uninhibited.

"Kissing you nearly made me lose control." He resisted the urge to run the pad of his thumb across her full bottom lip. The lip he'd sucked into his mouth and nibbled at hours earlier. "However, it didn't make me lose sight of our situation."

Pinning her with his gaze, Dylan balled his hands to keep from touching her. "I believe you, Lola, because as a detective, I encountered some of the best damn liars in the world," he said. "My gut tells me you're not one of them, and so far, it's never been wrong."

She rested a soft hand over his fist. The innocuous contact sent the warmth of awareness coursing through him. She looked down at their hands, and then returned her gaze to his face. Her expression made it clear she'd felt something, too.

"I've traveled the world and encountered a lot of people, but right here, right now, I think you, Dylan Cooper, are one of the very sweetest."

Clearing his throat, Dylan pulled his hand away and threw open the driver's side door. He stepped out of the truck and took a gulp of fresh, early evening air, removing himself from the close quarters of the truck cab.

He barely knew the woman, and already she controlled his mind. Moreover, Dylan wanted her, *badly*.

"Stay here," he ordered. "I'm going to take a look at the alleged crime scene." He spoke gruffly, knowing if she weren't a suspect, he'd attempt to do what she'd suggested he was capable of moments after they'd met—melt the panties right off her.

Chapter 9

A woman with one toe in a jail cell should have better sense than to lust after a man with the power to make her next fashion statement a neon-orange jumpsuit.

Lola's eyes ignored the admonishment from her common sense and continued to ogle his firm backside as he bent over to inspect something on the ground. The fact that he wasn't a stripper should have squashed the urge to want to smack it again.

It didn't.

"Get ahold of yourself," she whispered, finally peeling her eyeballs off his behind. Her current reputation should be enough to make her not even think about hitting anything or anybody. Not to mention the longer she was hung up in this town, on what really amounted to a huge misunderstanding, the further she was from sitting in the guest-host seat on *America Live!*

Lola experienced a twinge of panic at the thought of blowing one of the best opportunities to come her way since she became the face of Espresso at sixteen years old. The best way to get her anxiety in check was by taking action, she thought, and sitting in this truck becoming all hot and bothered over a small town cop wasn't putting her any closer to her goal.

After jumping out of the vehicle, she walked over to Dylan. He was standing a few feet from the police cruiser Wilson had been driving before he passed out, taking photos of the road with his phone.

"Didn't I tell you to stay in the truck?" He didn't look up from his task.

"Seeing as though I'm the one with her future and possibly her freedom on the line, I need to do all I can to help."

Dylan blew out a breath, and Lola steeled herself, expecting him to give her a hard time.

"Okay, but stand back and don't touch anything." He faced her, but his expression was once again an unreadable mask, and his voice held the same brusque edge it had when he'd left the truck. "You shouldn't even be out here. The last thing I need is your compromising the scene."

"I won't," Lola promised, as she wondered what had prompted the abrupt change in him. It was as if she'd imagined the easy camaraderie they'd shared moments earlier inside the truck.

She looked on as he resumed taking pictures of the road. "Why are you taking photos of the ground?"

"This is dried blood," he replied. Then he pointed out two black, side-by-side streaks forming a U shape. "I believe this is the rubber from the heels of Wilson's shoes as you dragged him around to the passenger seat of your car."

Dylan paused and gave her a once-over. "How did you manage that, anyway? Wilson is on the lanky side, but you have a slight frame."

"Pilates classes." Lola patted the flat abs she achieved through six-days-a-week classes and replacing the majority of her meals with a vitamin-enhanced protein shake. "All power radiates from the core."

Dylan nodded, apparently satisfied with her answer. He followed the blood-and-rubber-streaked trail to the graveled side of the road.

"That's where he passed out." Lola gestured to the patch of bloodstained ground and weeds.

Dylan took a few more pictures of the scene, including the police cruiser, with his phone. She looked on as he shut the driver's side door of the cop car. "I think I've seen all there is to see out here."

"This proves I was only trying to help him." As she followed him back to his truck Lola looked pointedly at the trail the rubber from the young officer's shoes had left on the road.

Dylan opened the passenger side door for her. "It only confirms you dragged Wilson to your car and got him to the hospital, which we already knew." He rounded the truck and slid behind the wheel. "As far as his injury goes, it's still his word against yours, and he has a witness on his side."

They rode in silence. Lola stared out the window, watching the surrounding cornfields give way to the roads leading back to the small town. Deep down, she knew the truth would win out, and she'd be proved innocent. However, it appeared it was going to take more time, which she didn't have to spare if she was going to get to New York City in time.

What in the hell was she going to do?

She hadn't even noticed Dylan had pulled out his phone until she heard him talking to what she gleaned from his end of the conversation was the hospital.

"I know I called less than an hour ago, Avis, but just how long are these tests going to take?" His sigh indicated he hadn't gotten the answer he'd wanted. "No. She hasn't been arrested, but if you keep spreading that false rumor about me dancing naked you'll be the one in a jail cell."

Lola could hear the nurse's laugh through the phone's tiny speaker as Dylan ended the call. He touched the screen to make another one.

"I'm calling County Dispatch to send a sheriff's office deputy to—"

"You're arresting me and sending me to the county jail?" Lola sat bolt upright in the seat.

Dylan shook his head, and she slumped in relief. "I'm having them drive the cruiser to the station. Wilson's out of commission, and I can't drive two vehicles," he said. "The sheriff's office backs me up when I need a hand."

Minutes later, they were back at the police station. Lola chewed her bottom lip, trying to come up with her next move.

"I'll finish talking to Wilson once the doctors release him," Dylan said, shutting off the truck's engine. "I'll find out what really happened out there, and then hopefully, I can send you on your way."

Lola rubbed a hand down her face. "But I know what happened," she said. "This has just been so frustrating." She closed her eyes and dropped her head back on the seat. "I can't be stuck in Mayberry while my career goes down the tubes," she muttered, more to herself more than anyone else.

She felt his large hand on her thigh. "It's going to be okay."

"You don't know that for sure." Lola opened her eyes. She knew both his touch and words were meant to soothe her, and they did up to a point. However, no matter how drawn she felt to him, this man was essentially a stranger.

She stared absently at a campaign placard asking citizens to vote Roy Cooper for mayor, placed in one of the public safety building's windows. Daylight was dwindling, along with the hours she had to make it to New York and the beauty appointments she needed to put her on her A game by Monday.

"For what it's worth, I still believe your version of the incident," Dylan said.

Lola wanted to trust him, but right now she was

tired, frustrated and just plain fed up. They walked into the police side of the building, and she was relieved to see the crowd hadn't returned. The place was blessedly empty except for Marjorie, who was humming and arranging a vase of pink day lilies in the jail cell that looked more and more as if Lola would indeed be utilizing it. There was also an elderly woman standing at Dylan's desk with a picnic hamper in tow.

Lola thought of her earlier reference to the fictional small town of Mayberry from the classic television reruns her father had often watched when she was a kid. She rolled her eyes toward the ceiling and grunted as details of the sitcom came to mind. Right now, her life seemed to be unfolding as if she'd been dropped in the middle of an episode of the laid-back comedy.

Only it wasn't so funny.

"Let's see. First, I encounter the *scrawny, bumbling deputy* who l end up rushing to a hospital located in a *quaint small town*, only to meet the *dreamboat sheriff*, who makes any woman with a pulse wish for a bottomless box of condoms and a king-size bed to—" Lola began.

"Actually," Marjorie, who had emerged from the pink jail cell, interrupted. "Wilson is indeed bumbling, but isn't a deputy. He's a police officer." She adjusted her wireless telephone headset and jabbed a thumb in Dylan's direction. "The dreamboat here is the police chief, not the sheriff. Oh, I've never seen a bottomless box of condoms. Can I find them at Warehouse Club?"

Lola adjusted her heavy pink bag on her shoulder. "Just roll with me, Marjorie." She turned to the elderly woman stationed at Dylan's desk, who was staring at her openmouthed. Lola zeroed in on the picnic hamper. "So you must be Aunt Bea."

The gray-haired woman closed her mouth, and her eyes, which held an air of familiarity, narrowed. "Nope, but I've seen you on television," she said. "You're the lady from the commercials who's fallen and can't get up."

Lola scowled at the reference as she tried to remember where she'd seen those big brown eyes.

A smirk spread over the woman's crinkled face. "Or is it the commercial where you're snuggled up with the old guy who *can't get it up*?" She raised a gray eyebrow. "Well, not without a little chemical boost."

"Goodness, Mom," Dylan said.

Mom? Oh, crap, Lola thought. "She's your mother?"

"The one and only," he replied. "Lola Gray, meet Virginia Cooper."

Lola gulped. From referring to his mother as Aunt Bea to leaving no doubt as to exactly what she wanted to do with her son, the past few minutes of dialogue came roaring back in her head. Geez, maybe everyone was right, Lola thought, and she really did need to get a handle on her impulsiveness and her mouth.

She glanced at Dylan, who appeared more amused than annoyed, hoping he'd help her pull her foot out of her mouth.

"A bottomless box, huh?" A smile spread over those kissable lips.

His innuendo ignited tingles in her core, and Lola's imagination supplied possibilities that made the delicious sensation spread like wildfire. Naughty possibilities she should not be entertaining in front of his mother.

Pulling herself together, Lola gave him the side-eye to let him know he wasn't helping. "Look, Mrs. Cooper, I apologize about the Aunt Bea comment," she said finally. "It's been a long, frustrating day."

"Then I guess I got off easy." Virginia Cooper smiled sweetly, but Lola didn't miss how those eyes sparkled with devilment. "You could have challenged me to go toe-to-toe, like you did with Wilson, who I have to admit to wanting to pop upside the head myself a time or two."

"But I didn't..." Lola started the familiar refrain of trying to defend herself, *again*.

"Lighten up, slugger." The older woman laughed. "I'm only teasing you."

Lola attempted a smile. In another time or place, she would have gotten a kick out of the older woman's quick wit. However, she was presently preoccupied with finding a way to first get out of trouble, and then get back on the road.

Marjorie sniffed the air. Her gaze fixed on the picnic hamper on Dylan's desk. "Mmm," she moaned.

Lola stomach growled in agreement as the delectable smells coming from the wicker basket reached her nose, reminding her she hadn't had anything since a hastily eaten egg-white-and-vegetable omelet that morning.

"I'd already started cooking when I got your text message saying you'd be tied up with work and couldn't make it for dinner," Virginia told her son. "So I thought I'd bring it."

"That was *real considerate* of you," Dylan said. The words were laced with suspicion.

"Well, I had to meet the talk of Cooper's Place," his mother admitted. "My phone's been ringing off the hook, since you kicked half the town out of here earlier. The girls figured I could play the nepotism card to get the real scoop."

Dylan frowned. "Hate to cut your covert mission short, but I'm still working the case," he said. "Lola has an important job opportunity. If what she says is true, I don't want her to miss out on it on account of being a Good Samaritan."

Virginia Cooper's eyes widened as she looked from Dylan to Lola, before once again training them on her son. "So it's Lola, huh?" She fired off another question. "Since when are you so chummy with a suspect?"

"We are not chummy," Dylan insisted.

"I may have been born at night, son. But it wasn't last night," Virginia said. "Besides, I heard about you stripping down to your birthday suit over at the hospital."

Dylan frowned. "And you believed it?"

"Hey! I thought you said that was just a rumor," Marjorie chimed in.

"A ridiculous rumor you'd think my own mother wouldn't buy into." Dylan turned to Virginia. "I thought we were better than idle gossip, Mom," he chastised.

"And I thought I raised you better than to let your new friend here spank your fanny in public," his mother countered. "I nearly fell off my chair when Rosemary Moody called to ask if I knew my son was playing kinky *Fifty Shades of Grey* games, in a hospital waiting room of all places."

Lola felt her face flush at the memory, which the rumor mill had taken entirely out of context. "B-but it wasn't what you think, Mrs. Cooper," she stammered.

"I think the bottomless box of condoms you bragged about tells me everything I need to know, miss."

Dylan exhaled. "You're enjoying stirring the pot, aren't you?" he asked his mother.

Virginia let loose with the laugh she'd apparently been holding back. "Almost as much as I enjoy my social security check hitting the bank on the first of the month."

"Speaking of pots…" Marjorie cleared her throat loudly. "Any other time I'd love to hear a blow-by-blow of how Ms. Gray and the chief get their freak on, but I'm starving and whatever is in that basket is calling my name."

"We were *not* getting our freak on," Dylan said.

Too bad, Lola thought, and then hurriedly glanced around to make sure the words hadn't tumbled out of her mouth.

"Has the hospital called about Wilson yet?" Dylan asked Marjorie.

"I touched base with them fifteen minutes ago. They're not done with him, and Avis says us calling over there every five minutes isn't going to make them go any faster."

"Then we might as well eat," Virginia said.

Opening the large basket, Dylan's mother pulled out a plastic cake carrier. She removed the domed lid, unveiling a white-frosted cake garnished with candied lemon slices.

"Oh, my God, lemonade layer cake." Marjorie clasped her hands together in the prayer position. "I bid seventy-five bucks on one of these at the library fund-raiser and still didn't win. No way I'm going to miss out on having at least two pieces, maybe three."

"My mother, my cake," Dylan argued.

Marjorie snorted. "Not anymore."

Meanwhile, Lola's stomach rumbled as Virginia continued to unload the basket, turning her son's desk into a makeshift buffet table. Lola stared longingly at the fried chicken, macaroni and cheese, and rolls glazed with what appeared to be both honey and butter. It all smelled heavenly, and Lola suspected she was drooling.

"I'll get the paper plates and napkins," Marjorie volunteered.

Lola requested bottled water when Dylan went to retrieve soft drinks from the vending machine. Thanking him, she twisted the cap off the bottle and noticed Marjorie arranging a fourth place setting on the desk. Lola shook her head. "I'm not having anything," she said.

Three pairs of eyes stared at her incredulously.

"Why not?" Virginia asked. "And don't tell me you're not hungry because the sounds coming from your stomach remind me of a monster truck revving up for a race."

Sighing, Lola allowed herself one last look at the food as her well-honed willpower kicked into place. "My diet is extremely regimented. Unfortunately, none of this amazing-looking food is allowed."

"You're so thin. Surely a little bit won't hurt," Virginia said.

Lola shook her head as her stomach roared in protest. "The camera adds at least ten pounds. I can't afford any slipups. Especially now."

"I'll take her share." Marjorie took her gaze off her already loaded plate to eyeball the cake.

"Our grocery store is on the small side, but if you need something special I can see if they have it," Dylan offered.

Lola retrieved a plastic blender bottle and packet of protein powder from her purse. "No, water is all I need."

The mouthwatering aromas coming from the desk seemed to intensify as she filled the blender bottle with water and dumped in the contents of the packet. She scowled at the three of them as they began to eat, knowing she had no right to be annoyed. Not that they'd even noticed. They were all too busy devouring the food on their plates.

Lola shook the contents of the bottle harder to blend them, then drank deeply. The chalky aftertaste of the protein-and-vitamin shake she substituted for two of her three meals a day insulted her deprived taste buds.

It'll be worth it when you walk into that television studio on Monday svelte and on your A game, she reminded herself.

Lola raised the bottle to her lips again, but paused when she saw they were moving on to the cake. No way was she going to stand there torturing herself while they ate that gorgeous dessert. She stalked off to drink her shake in peace.

"Where are you going?" Dylan and Marjorie asked simultaneously.

"To my cell." Lola walked into the storage room slash jail cell and clanged the old-fashioned door shut. She plopped down on the cot and sipped her shake. "Enjoy your cake."

"So how do you like your cell?" Marjorie called out. Lola could see her expectant smile from across the room. "I hope I didn't go overboard on the pink."

"It's lovely," she replied in a monotone voice.

"You do realize you aren't under arrest. At this point, you're only being detained," Dylan said. "You can drink your meal or shake or whatever that is out here with the rest of us."

"The up-close-and-personal view of you all stuffing your faces, when I can't have any, may drive me to do something that will keep me in here for real," Lola said.

She heard a loud huff from Virginia. "Good Lord, stop being a drama queen and have a slice of cake before these two eat it all." The older woman glanced at her son and Marjorie, and then shook her head. "You'd think they'd never seen food before."

Dylan put down his fork, which he hadn't done since they'd commenced eating. "Give Lola a break, Mom. If her version of what happened to Wilson is true, then she's been extremely patient with this entire town."

His mother blinked. "You believe her, don't you?"

Lola watched Dylan nod once, and her heart did a tiny flip inside her chest. She took another sip from her shake and leaned against the pink pillow she'd propped up against the wall.

"She also has a big job waiting on her in New York."

Virginia looked across the room at Lola. "But I thought you already had a job modeling for Espresso?"

"You've known who I was this entire time," Lola said.

"Of course. I'd know your face anywhere. I've been a loyal Espresso Cosmetics customer for years." Virginia's tone was matter-of-fact. "I went to one of their events in Nashville over thirty years ago, and Selena Sinclair Gray made up my face personally. At the time, I thought she was one of the most glamorous and the most beautiful women I'd ever seen. I wanted to look just like her."

"So did I," Lola said softly, at the mention of her late mother.

"You do," Virginia assured her.

Lola smiled at the older woman, surprised she'd even heard her from across the room.

"So why are you looking for a job in New York when you already have one with your own people?" Virginia asked.

"Geez, Mom. You're as nosy as everyone else in this town." Dylan shook his head as he cut into the slice of cake on his plate with a fork. He shoved a bite into his mouth.

"There's nothing wrong with asking a question or two." Virginia shot him a look. "At least I can keep my clothes on when I'm talking to her."

"Thank goodness," Dylan grumbled.

Lola snickered, but noticed he didn't even bother to deny the inaccurate rumor.

Undeterred, his mother pressed on. "So did your family fire you after that big flap on the airplane?"

"Yep, how'd you guess?" Lola had told only Dylan, and unlike everyone else in town, he didn't gossip.

"Just put two and two together." Virginia shrugged. "Besides, with all the press you're getting lately, you'd be a better spokesman for boxing gloves and emergency rooms than makeup."

Lola shrugged. "It's better than my face being associated with hemorrhoid cream."

Dylan froze, his fork poised midair. "Hey! Some of us are trying to eat here."

"We're just...um, what's that saying again?" His mother paused and then snapped her fingers. "Oh, yeah. Lola and I just like to keep it real."

"Yes, we do," Lola agreed. She also couldn't help

thinking about how much she liked the Coopers, both of them. The mother was a hoot, and the son… Lola stole a glance at him and couldn't suppress a dreamy sigh.

Dylan Cooper was a bona fide hunk, but that was only a small part of his appeal. Rock-solid and supportive, his quiet strength embraced her like a hug. Her looks and her strong personality didn't intimidate him. Nor did hearing about the situations she seemed to continuously get herself into annoy him.

Lola had known Dylan for a few hours, yet already she felt she could relax and be herself around him—quirks and all.

Her mind drifted back to the kiss they had shared earlier. It had turned her on for sure, but more than that, in those few minutes she'd spent in his arms she had felt more at home than she'd felt in a long time. Then Lola realized she was in another jam, because she was falling for this town's police chief.

The sound of her name roused her from her reverie and the inane notions running through her head. She didn't even know Dylan Cooper. Not really. The idea of her falling for him was just plain silly. Or was it?

"I was asking you about your job opportunity," Virginia said.

Shaking off ridiculous thoughts of Dylan being anything more to her than a helpful guy she wouldn't mind seeing *and touching* naked, Lola proceeded to fill his mother and Marjorie in on the call from her agent. She also found herself confiding in them about the humiliating way she'd been fired and replaced by a drag queen.

The dispatcher cut a third slice of lemonade cake and placed it on her plate. "Wow, that must be one good-looking man."

Lola recalled Freddy Finch's head shot. "He's gorgeous," she deadpanned.

"Back to your *America Live!* appearance," Virginia said. "It's one of my favorite shows. I watch it every morning while I eat breakfast."

"Me, too," Marjorie chimed in over a mouthful of cake. "Can't we just let her go, if she promises to come back?"

Dylan shook his head. "The crime she's been accused of is too serious, and two people claim she did it."

"What people?" Virginia asked.

"Jeb for one," Dylan replied. "He claims to have seen the entire incident while he was out on his tractor."

Virginia dismissed the name with a wave of her hand. "Jeb Dixon can barely see the shoes on his feet, let alone Old Mill Road from his property line."

"What the...?" Lola's ears perked up and she raised her back off the plush pink pillow. "I couldn't even make out the person driving the tractor. There's no way they could have seen me."

"Wilson also indicated she attacked him, but he was vague," Dylan said.

"I heard he had a head injury. He could be confused," Marjorie said.

"Or…" Virginia tapped her fingertip against her lips. "Well, this is just a thought, but the young man is the butt of a lot of jokes around here. Maybe he's embarrassed to say what really happened out there, and it's easier to let everyone believe Lola waylaid him."

"Come on." Marjorie's tone was incredulous.

Lola was inclined to share the dispatcher's opinion. Virginia's notion seemed like a stretch. Lola was taken aback when Dylan supported his mother's theory.

"That's exactly what I think is going on here, Mom," he said. "Lola's reputation is a smokescreen that shifts the attention off Wilson and onto her. Instead of folks laughing at him, he's seen as courageous for being ambushed by a woman rumored to be a menace. When anybody who's spent any time with her would know that's just a crock. If anything, I believe she's the hero in this situation."

Lola's heart did that flip-flop thing in her chest again. While it was ridiculous to think she was falling for Dylan so soon after meeting him, she did like him—a lot. She also appreciated the faith he had in her.

"Then why—" Virginia began.

Dylan cut her off, apparently already knowing his mother's question. "Because at this point it's Jeb and Wilson's word against Lola's. Our cruiser isn't equipped with a video camera and the evidence is negligible. While I'm hesitant to arrest her, I can't let her go. Not yet." He exhaled. "Our best bet is to get what I believe is the truth out of Wilson as soon as he's done at the hospital."

Virginia banged a fist on the desk, startling the entire room. "We can't just wait around on Wilson. We've got to take action now. Lola is supposed to be on *America Live!* Monday morning, dammit." Her voice trembled with indignation. "This is her chance to let the country get to know her, beyond all the ridiculous gossip she attracts. Not to mention show that family of hers up for thinking a drag queen is a better spokesperson than Lola for Espresso."

Lola appreciated the older woman's fervor. She trusted Dylan and his approach was logical, but wished there was something they could do to move the process along. Even if they managed to get it cleared up this evening, she'd probably have to find a hotel and stay the night in Cooper's Place. She was exhausted, and there was still over five hundred miles left between her and New York City.

"I realize how important this is to Lola," Dylan said. "But I can't let my personal feelings in this case interfere with doing my job."

Marjorie snapped her fingers. "Hold on, I think there's something else we can try, but I don't know…" she hedged. "It's kind of a stretch."

"Anything," Lola pleaded. Time wasn't on her side.

"We could hold a hearing in Mayor's Court," the dispatcher said. "I know it doesn't convene until Wednesday, but perhaps we could call a special session." She shrugged. "For tomorrow morning, maybe? It would give us time for the mayor to agree to it."

"That's a fabulous idea." The sound of Virginia's clap reverberated throughout the room as she excitedly clasped her hands. "To heck with waiting until tomorrow. I'll call Roy right now. I think we could have all the players at city hall for an emergency session of Mayor's Court within the hour."

"No," Dylan said firmly. "Absolutely, not."

"Why not?" both Virginia and Marjorie asked, echoing the question going through Lola's head.

Dylan stood as he frowned at his mother and the dispatcher. "For one thing, I'm not even sure if it's legal. Only traffic cases and misdemeanors are handled in Mayor's Court."

"The so-called crime happened in Cooper's Place, and we can handle it right here in Cooper's Place," his mother said. *"Right now."*

Marjorie stood. She sided up to Virginia and draped her arm around the older woman's shoulder. "I agree with you."

Dylan cleared his throat. "Secondly, this is a bad idea for reasons the two of you should already know." He heaved a sigh, as he appeared to measure his next words. "I love my uncle, but that doesn't hide the fact that he can be an ass."

Lola blinked. It was the first time she'd heard the police chief swear. So she figured his uncle must be a pretty big one.

Virginia shrugged. "I can't argue the part about him being an ass."

"Me, either," Marjorie readily agreed.

"Still, it's a shot at getting Lola out of here and on

my television Monday morning, and I vote we should take it," Virginia said.

"It would be a bad move," Dylan warned. "The hospital should be done with those tests on Wilson soon. We just need to be patient a little longer."

Lola watched as the older woman rested a hand on her son's arm. "But it's not your future on the line, it's Lola's. Don't you think we should leave it up to her?"

They all turned to the jail cell. She did trust Dylan's opinion, but she also needed to get out of here tonight. Marjorie and Virginia's idea sounded as if it would help her achieve her goal quicker than his would.

Standing, Lola gripped the jail cell's old-fashioned bars. "I want my night in court."

Chapter 10

He'd called it right.

This truly was a bad idea, but Dylan hadn't realized just how awful until it began to play out before his eyes. He closed them briefly and pinched the bridge of his nose as he sat on the front row of a packed house at city hall for an unprecedented hearing in Mayor's Court.

He'd already told the court what he'd gleaned from the evidence he'd collected, and indicated he believed the only thing Lola Gray was guilty of was speeding.

Now Jeb Dixon was at the podium giving his account of what had happened to Officer Todd Wilson on Old Mill Road. Mayor Roy Cooper was in a cantankerous mood because he was missing the baseball game on television, and Lola wasn't doing herself any favors.

"I've already warned you twice, young lady." The mayor, seated at the dais where he usually presided over city council meetings, picked up his gavel and pointed it in Lola's direction. "Keep interrupting these proceedings and you're going to find yourself in contempt of court."

"But that's not what happened at all." Lola continued to challenge Jeb's rambling, vague version of the story.

"That may be so, but I need to hear what he has to say just the same," Roy said. "So plant your backside in your seat and keep quiet, before you get on my bad side and I hold you in contempt."

Dylan recognized the warning tone in his uncle's directive. As a kid, it had stopped him dead in his tracks. He hoped Lola had the good sense to heed it, because Roy Cooper's bite was always worse than his bark.

Lola returned to her seat on the pew-style bench, bracketed by him and his mother. Dylan felt the tension trapped between his shoulders ebb. He looked down at her trembling hand resting against her thigh and resisted the urge to reach out and cover it with his. The instinct to comfort her came as naturally to him as his next breath. Still, it wouldn't be appropriate.

As a small-town police chief, he knew the respect of his fellow citizens was vital. So was their confidence in his sense of fairness. He couldn't be perceived as giving Lola special treatment because of her celebrity status. All he wanted was to give a woman he believed had tried to do the right thing by rushing his officer to the emergency room a chance to clear her name.

Dylan doubted tonight's hearing would achieve that goal.

"Now where were we before being so rudely interrupted, *again*?" Roy's eyes narrowed in disapproval at Lola, before he swiveled in his high-backed chair toward his long-time fishing buddy, Jeb, leaning against the podium.

A cell phone rang out and everyone glanced around nervously, curious to see who'd been foolish enough to ignore the signs outside the room warning to silence all phones before entering. Dylan watched as Jeb fished an ancient flip phone out of the pocket of his plaid shirt.

"Hello. Hello?" The farmer's bellow bounced off the walls of the room.

"Put that phone away, Jeb," the mayor scolded.

"What did you say?" Jeb shouted into the small phone. "Speak up. Roy's yelling, and I can't hear a thing." He jammed a finger in his free ear. "That's better. I can hear you now. Nope, I'm missing *The Price is Right* prime-time special tonight, but Darcy is recording it, so don't tell me who won Plinko. You know it's my favorite."

Roy banged his gavel. "Jeb!"

Turning his back on his friend, Jeb continued to speak loudly into the phone, treating the entire room to his side of the conversation whether or not they wanted to hear it.

"Oh, I'm down in Mayor's Court telling everyone how the lady from the TV who beat up the folks on that plane knocked out one of the town's cops." Oblivious to where he was and everyone around him, the farmer continued the call. "The rookie, of course. You know the chief. That Dylan Cooper's *one big mudda*...not even those lumberjack-sized Henderson brothers could take him on, and there's three of them."

Jeb stopped talking for a beat, and turned to the front row, where Dylan sat with Lola. His eyes widened before he squinted at them through the thick lenses of his glasses. He stroked the whiskers on his chin with his free hand and grinned. "Stripped him buck naked and spanked him, right in the hospital waiting room, eh?"

Dylan tensed. This ridiculous rumor had taken on a life of its own, and it was beyond time he put stop to it. He was about to stand when he felt Lola's hand on his arm. She shook her head, and Dylan instantly understood. Explaining what had really happened wouldn't stop the inaccurate rumors. It would only continue to fuel them.

Besides, their goal was to get her out of this mess, not embroil her in another one.

"Jeb Dixon, hang up that phone right now!" Roy shouted, and his friend finally complied. "Now finish explaining what you saw out on Old Mill Road."

Jeb's thick glasses had slid down his nose, and he

adjusted them with his forefinger. "Well, I figured she must have decked him, because one minute she was in the car and the next Ms. Gray was standing over poor Wilson."

"He's lying!" Lola practically leaped from her seat.

"Am not," Jeb argued. "I'm what they call on those television court shows an eyewitness."

Lola folded her arms over her chest. "Eyewitness? Humph. More like a *lie-witness*."

Laughter erupted in the courtroom slash city council chambers, followed by the buzz of conversation.

"Order! Order!" Roy snatched up his gavel again and slammed it against its sound block repeatedly. "Be quiet or I'll clear the room."

A hush fell over the spectators. No one wanted to miss one of the most exciting things to happen in Cooper's Place in years.

"I warned you twice, Ms. Gray. I'm swiftly approaching the end of my patience with you," Roy said.

"With me?" Lola asked incredulously, and threw her arms in the air. "I'm already at the end of my patience, Mayor. In fact, I'm just plain fed up. I've already been railroaded twice today, and I'm not just going to sit back and let it happen again." She pointed at Jeb. "This guy is either mistaken or just a big, fat liar."

Once again, the din of conversation rose in the background.

"Whatcha going do, Lola, wallop him, too?" someone yelled.

Dylan felt a nudge at his side and turned to his mother. She gestured for him to lean in.

"This might not have been a good idea, after all," she whispered in his ear.

He pulled back and frowned. "You think?" Sarcasm dripped off the rhetorical question.

Roy slammed his gavel so hard it fell apart, leaving him angrily clutching the handle. "That's it, you're now in contempt of my court, young lady," Roy said. "You may trash hotel rooms and run roughshod over airlines in other places, but I don't tolerate bad behavior in my court. Not from you. Not from anyone."

"Whatever." Lola snorted as she returned to her seat.

Dylan hoped having what she thought was the last word in the verbal sparring wouldn't come back to haunt her. This time he didn't hesitate to place his large hand over Lola's smaller one, but instead of comfort and support, he hoped it conveyed a silent message of restraint.

He'd gently squeezed her hand twice when he felt her about to spring up to dispute Jeb's testimony again. To his relief she'd remained seated. His uncle had already found her in contempt, and who knew how that would play out?

A few minutes later, Roy excused Jeb from the podium. "Has Officer Wilson arrived yet?" he asked.

"Not yet, but he's on his way," the town clerk replied.

The mayor looked at his watch. "I don't have all

night," he said. "Ms. Gray, I'll hear your side of the story next. Wilson can have his turn after you."

Lola took to the podium and was sworn in by the town clerk. For the next ten minutes, she relayed to the mayor and half the town her account of the events on the deserted road. Dylan looked on and tried to gauge how her statement was coming across to his uncle, as well as the residents filling the gallery.

"Let me make sure I have this straight." Roy Cooper frowned at Lola. "You expect us to believe the unlikely story that Officer Wilson took one look at your injured hand and passed out?"

Dylan watched Lola's lips tighten. "That's exactly what I expect you to believe, Mr. Mayor, because it's what happened." She pushed the words through clenched teeth. "He took one look at my bleeding hand, whispered the word *blood* and dropped like a rock."

Roy grunted and crossed his arms over his chest.

Dylan didn't consider himself an impulsive man. He thought about what he said and what he did before speaking or taking action. However, right now, he was having difficulty staying in his seat and not challenging this proceeding. If you could call it that.

His uncle Roy appeared to already have it fixed in his head that Lola was guilty and should be charged and arrested, and nothing was going to change his mind.

Not Dylan's statement, not the report of the doctor who had examined Lola, nor Jeb's dubious account.

But he's not the only one who's biased.

Kissing Lola replayed through Dylan's head. It was one of the few times in life he had been impulsive, and although he shouldn't have kissed her back, he had no regrets.

Still, the constant desire to kiss her again hadn't skewed his judgment. Every cell in his body told him Lola wasn't the culprit here. If anything, she was the victim, of hearsay and her own reputation.

"Approach the bench and show me this alleged injury of yours." Roy examined Lola's hand and sniffed. "Looks like nothing more than a scratch to me. I can barely see it."

Dylan abruptly stood. "But you saw the hospital report," he said. "I'll grant you it's a small cut, but it was indeed bleeding when she brought Wilson to the emergency room."

"Yep, she was bleeding all right."

Dylan turned around to see Avis standing in the back of the packed room, still wearing her uniform. Their outbursts had sent the rest of the spectators into a tizzy.

His gavel broken, Roy banged his fist against the dais repeatedly. "Quiet!" he shouted over the din, and then scowled. "Don't tell me how to do my job, nephew."

Dylan matched his disapproving look with one of his own. "Then do it justly, uncle."

"Keep it up and you'll be found in contempt, too. Just like your new girlfriend here."

"She is not my girlfriend," Dylan said firmly. Although, like his uncle, everyone in town seemed to have their minds made up on that subject, too.

His face and jaw clenched, Dylan managed to keep seated through the rest of Lola's stint at the podium answering the mayor's slanted questions. His mother and Marjorie harrumphed at several of them.

He could feel the fight seeping out of Lola as she took her seat next to him. Their eyes met, something clicked between them and they automatically reached for each other's hand. Dylan couldn't explain it, nor did he try to fight it.

However, he would fight for her even though he knew nothing could ever come of their attraction. Her future was awaiting her in New York, and he'd do whatever he had to do to make sure she made it there.

They were still gazing into each other's eyes when every other head in the room swiveled toward the door in the back of the room. Dylan turned around.

Wilson.

The spectators broke out in applause. Several men stood and patted him on the back. The very people who had poked fun at Wilson most of his life were now greeting him as a hero. It was the most respect the young officer had received since he'd taken the job, and unfortunately, Dylan didn't believe he'd earned it.

"That poor kid. Beaten on the side of the road and left for dead," a woman said.

"Give me a break," Lola whispered.

The mayor spoke into the microphone mounted to

the dais. "Are you feeling up to giving us your side of the story, Officer Wilson?"

"I think so," the rookie officer said hesitantly.

"Well, come on up to the podium or do you need the clerk to get you a chair?"

"My tests came back fine, and I've been released from the hospital," Wilson said. "I'm all right with the podium."

Dylan caught his eye as the rookie officer walked up the aisle. Wilson spotted Lola seated next to him and averted his gaze. The young man stared at the floor until he reached the podium. Everything about his body language said he was weighed down by the guilt of his lies. Dylan was sure it would take only a few minutes of questioning for him to get to the truth.

It had been the option he'd have preferred rather than Lola taking her chances in Mayor's Court. While Dylan was sure any decision reached at this sham of a hearing could easily be overturned or tossed out entirely, that couldn't happen until the opening of business on Monday morning. Too late for Lola's scheduled appearance on *America Live!*

Dylan stood. "Mr. Mayor," he said, addressing his uncle by his title, "I'd like to request a short recess to give me an opportunity to finish taking Officer Wilson's statement. We were interrupted at the hospital before I completed the interview."

His uncle leaned back in the leather chair as he appeared to consider it. The tension resettled between Dylan's shoulders as he awaited the older man's decision.

"Hmm," Roy murmured, and then shook his head. "I've heard what I need to know. I just need Officer Wilson to confirm a few things, so I'll be asking the questions."

"But—" Dylan began.

"This matter is before my court now. You're officially off the case." His uncle looked from him to Lola. "And in light of your obvious bias toward Ms. Gray, we'll call a county deputy to handle any arrest. So have a seat, Chief Cooper."

Dylan did as he was told as the beginning of an idea began to take shape in his head. He was a city employee, so the mayor was indeed his boss. However, Dylan wasn't done with this case. Not yet.

He looked at Lola. Worry creased her face and she was biting her lip as she listened to his uncle ask Wilson a couple of amenable questions and accept his evasive answers.

"What a crock," Virginia grumbled.

It earned her a side-eye from his uncle, but not the verbal dressing-down everyone else who'd gotten on the wrong side of him this evening had received. Not even Roy wanted to tangle with his sister-in-law.

The mayor returned his attention to the podium. "One last question, son. Do you have a phobia where blood is concerned?"

Dylan looked on as Wilson opened his mouth to speak, but exhaled a breath instead. He got the impression the rookie was about to tell the truth. However, a titter of laughter sounded in a corner of the room and quickly spread through the crowd of spectators until nearly everyone had joined in.

The young man's demeanor abruptly changed, and Dylan knew he wasn't about to admit to something that would rob him of his newly found respect and possibly make him, once again, the butt of jokes.

Glancing at Lola, Dylan could feel the frustration radiating off her as words from earlier came back to him.

"I've already been railroaded twice today, I'm not just going to sit back and let it happen again."

Neither was he, Dylan thought. "It's an easy question." There were gasps in the audience at his outburst. "Either you have a blood phobia or you don't."

"Um... I... That doesn't make any sense," the rookie stammered.

"You sure about that?"

"Dylan Cooper." His uncle angrily called his name. "Come up here, right now."

Dylan shoved a hand in his pants pocket, stood and walked the few steps to the dais.

"Just what do you think you're doing?" the mayor asked.

"Trying to get an answer to your question," Dylan said. "An honest one."

Using one hand, still in his pocket, Dylan flicked open the tiny utility knife he'd confiscated at the elementary school that morning. He flinched as he pressed the small blade into the heel of his palm.

Dylan pulled his hand from his pocket and held it out. Blood oozed from a small cut as he approached the podium and held his palm a few inches from the young man's face.

"Sit down, Chief Cooper. I'm asking the questions here," Roy said.

Dylan ignored him.

"Again, Officer Wilson, do you have a phobia about…" Dylan didn't get a chance to finish his question.

"Blood."

Wilson stumbled backward and his eyes rolled up in his head. Dylan swiftly moved in and caught the young officer before he hit the ground. Then he effortlessly picked him up, tossed his limp body over his shoulder and carried him to the dais. He sat him in one of the vacant leather chairs reserved for members of the city council.

His uncle stared at him slack-jawed.

"You have your answer—now you have no choice but to put an end to this," Dylan told the older man.

They faced off a few minutes, and then his uncle reluctantly pulled the microphone toward him. "The court finds Officer Todd Wilson was not assaulted. Therefore no charges will be filed against Lola Gray, and this matter is closed."

Dylan exhaled a long sigh of relief.

"Need a bandage, Chief?" Avis had rushed up to the dais. She looked at the cut on his hand.

"I'm fine. It's only a prick. Just make sure Wilson is okay," Dylan told the nurse as he inclined his head toward the unconscious officer. "And when he wakes up, tell him he's fired."

Lola.

Dylan pivoted to look for her, only to see her bull-dozing toward him, a huge grin on her beautiful face. In her excitement, she launched herself at him, and he swept her up as she leaped into his arms.

He felt her arms encircle his neck as she wrapped those long legs around his waist.

"Thank you," she said. "But your hand—"

Dylan cut off her question, capturing her lips in a celebratory kiss. He held her close, and his tongue delved into her mouth. Every movement was long, slow and deliberate.

Dylan was a man of few words. However, he wanted to show her this kiss was no accident, nor a case of him getting carried away like before. His first taste of her had left him with an all-day craving, and now it was time to satisfy it.

He continued to take his time exploring her mouth. A groan sounded deep in her throat, and he felt her hands at his chest. They applied gentle pressure and she wrenched her mouth away.

"Dylan," she whispered, glancing around them.

He followed her gaze, taking in the crowd of spectators, most of whom were still seated. Every mouth was moving, talking animatedly about this evening. Dylan suspected the event would be the main gossip for weeks. Long after Lola was gone.

He shoved the thought from his mind. Although he knew she'd be eager to see the last of Cooper's Place, he didn't want to think about it. Not yet.

Returning his focus to the present and the

woman in his arms, Dylan saw a glimmer of self-consciousness cross her face.

Lola unwrapped her limbs from around his body. "Kissing me in public isn't a good idea. You're their police chief, and up until a few minutes ago, I was a suspect. Folks might think there's something going on between us."

Isn't there? Dylan nearly asked. Although they hadn't acted upon it, and he'd been denying it all day to himself and everyone else, there was definitely something going on between him and Lola Gray. An electric current of attraction he'd felt from the moment he first saw her. And every time she looked at him, Dylan knew she felt it, too.

"Right now, I'm not concerned with what anyone thinks. You've been cleared." He glanced at the clock behind the dais. "And unless there's an emergency, I'm officially off duty."

Lola briefly consulted the same clock. "I feel like we should celebrate, but it's late and I need to hit the sack so I can get back on the road in the morning."

"Maybe there's a way for us to do both." Dylan raised a brow. "Hit the sack and celebrate."

A wicked smile spread across her mouth, the same smile she'd worn when she'd thought he was a stripper and had told him to get naked. "Tell me more."

Dylan brought his lips to her ear and in a low voice only she could hear proceeded to tell her exactly how he thought they should celebrate.

Lola pulled back and faced him. She raised a brow. "For that long, huh?"

"And that hard," Dylan guaranteed.

"Then let's say good-night to your mother and Marjorie and get the hell out of here."

Lola dropped her voice to a sexy growl and touched a fingertip to his chest. "This time, I'll strip you myself. Then I'm gonna ride you like a…"

Dylan licked his lips in anticipation of her stated intentions, but feedback from the microphone at the dais drowned them out. The squawking noise, along with the pounding of his uncle's fist, drew everyone's attention to the front of the room.

"Quiet!" The mayor shushed the audience with one word.

What in the world was his uncle up to now? Dylan wondered. Nothing good, that was for sure.

"We're not done here," the mayor said. "So have a seat, Ms. Gray, and stop making a spectacle of yourself with my nephew."

Dylan held her in place, firmly against him. "Lola's not been charged with assaulting Wilson, so she's free to go."

"Yes and *no*." A spiteful grin spread over his uncle's face. "I found her in contempt of court, and she's most certainly not free to go."

Hushed whispers from the section reserved for spectators filled his ears, and Dylan could feel Lola trembling in his arms.

"This is bullshit," she shouted at the dais.

Roy Cooper's mouth dropped open, and he looked down at his nephew. "Are you going to let her talk to me like that? I'm your flesh and blood. She's just passing through town."

"Considering the way she's been treated by this town and this court, Lola is absolutely right. The very least we can do is let her be on her way."

His uncle's scowl deepened. "Fortunately, I'm the mayor here, and I have the final say, not you." He glared at Lola. "Ms. Gray, in light of the contempt you showed for Mayor's Court and this evening's proceedings, I'm ordering you to serve eight hours of community service commencing at seven o'clock Monday morning, when you'll report to the public works department for further instructions. Be prepared to work *hard*."

The whispers in the room turned to grumbles.

"But I have a job in New York on Monday."

"You should have thought about that before you ran that sassy mouth of yours and ignored my repeated warnings," the mayor said. "You will start serving your sentence at the appointed hour, or I'll have a warrant issued for your arrest. You'll be tracked down and hauled directly to the county jail." Roy snorted. "And they won't be nearly as accommodating to *your needs* as my nephew has apparently been."

"Just let me go for a few days, Mr. Mayor," Lola pleaded. "I promise I'll come back and serve every single one of those hours starting Tuesday morning."

"My decision is final, Ms. Gray," Roy said.

"But this job, it's vital to my career and—"

"Allow me to toss out a word you used earlier." The mayor cut off her plea. With an exaggerated shrug, he mimicked Lola's voice. *"Whatever."*

Chapter 11

Lola had needed time to think, *alone*.

It was the reason she hadn't spent the night before where she'd really wanted to—in Dylan Cooper's bed. Instead, she'd come home with his mother, whose seasonal bed-and-breakfast was the closest thing the small town had to a hotel.

Only Lola hadn't gotten much thinking done. Weariness from the fiasco of a day, which had only one bright spot, had quickly claimed her, and she'd fallen asleep atop the plush duvet seconds after being shown to her room.

She awoke in the middle of the night to find her suitcase sitting near the door. A note from Dylan, her bright spot, was stuck to the handle, stating he'd borrowed her keys from her bag to retrieve both the suitcase and her Mustang from the hospital parking lot. The note also mentioned a conversation with his lawyer, who was confident she could get an emergency stay of the mayor's order over the weekend that would ensure Lola could be at the television studio Monday morning.

All she had to do was say the word.

Still too exhausted to consider her options, Lola had pulled her pajamas from the suitcase, changed and crawled back into bed. She'd fallen asleep again immediately. Clutching Dylan's note in her hand, Lola dreamed of the sensual promises he'd whispered in her ear.

Hours later, the tantalizing aroma of cinnamon roused Lola from a deep slumber, along with the sounds of male voices coming from the floor below. Very demanding, very familiar voices.

"Is she here?"

"She's upstairs," she heard Dylan answer. His deep baritone brought to mind the things they'd done in her dreams, and made her wish she were waking up in his bed this morning. "However, Lola's had a trying time yesterday and needs her rest," Dylan said.

"What my sister needs is to bring her troublemaking behind home to Nashville."

Cole.

"Oh, crap." Lola threw back the covers and bounded out of bed. She snatched her pink robe from the suitcase she'd left open on a chair.

"Keep your voices down. We've already told you she's sleeping." Virginia's annoyed tone carried up the staircase.

"Then get her up," Cole ordered. "We're getting her out of this hick town *now.*"

An irate voice that sounded like her brother-in-law's agreed with Cole. This wasn't good, Lola thought. Not at all.

She jammed her arms into the sleeves of her robe as the anger level of the voices coming from downstairs continued to escalate. All but one voice, she noticed. It maintained its resoluteness, while remaining cool and unruffled.

"How about you two calm down," Dylan said. "You say you've been driving all night. Then have a cup of coffee and enjoy a couple of my mom's cinnamon rolls while you wait for Lola to get up, because *no one is going to disturb her.*"

"I don't want coffee. I don't want a cinnamon roll. And I will not calm down," Cole thundered.

Forgoing her slippers, Lola ran out of the bedroom and started down the hallway leading to the staircase. A framed photograph on the wall caught her eye, and she stopped short.

Lola stared at the photo of Dylan dressed in a different police uniform than the one he'd worn yesterday. He stood ramrod straight as a medal was pinned to his broad chest. She lowered her gaze to the ornate certificate mounted in the same frame. It was dated three years ago. Running a fingertip across the glass, she softly read parts of it aloud.

"Awarded to Detective Dylan Cooper by the Chicago Police Department for distinguished acts of bravery in the protection of life…"

"Lola!" she heard Cole bellow. "Wake up, and get down here!"

At the sound of her name echoing throughout the house, Lola bolted down the hallway and took the stairs barefoot, two at a time. She burst into the kitchen to find Cole and Dylan facing off on opposite ends of it, while Virginia and Ethan sat at a large table in the center of the room eating giant cinnamon rolls slathered in cream-cheese icing.

Dylan caught sight of her first. He placed the coffee mug in his hand on the counter he was leaning against, and an easy smile spread across his mouth. "Morning," he said. Those brown eyes pinned her with a look that made her wonder if he knew exactly what she'd dreamed he'd done with that very mouth last night.

Lola flushed down to her bare feet at the thought.

"It's about time you got up," Cole snapped, bringing her out of her reverie. "Get dressed. We're taking you home."

Lola blinked, as her mind first reconciled the fact that Cole and Ethan were in Cooper's Place, and then that her older brother had started in on her without as much as a hello.

"What are you two doing here?" She looked from one to the other and then to the clock on the stove. "At six o'clock in the morning? And why are you being so rude to Dylan and Virginia?"

Cole continued barking orders as if she hadn't uttered a word. "Ethan will drive your Mustang, and you can ride with me."

Her brother-in-law inclined his head in her direction, his mouth stuffed with cinnamon roll.

Surprise morphed into annoyance as Lola folded her arms across her chest. "I asked what y'all were doing here," she repeated. "And how did you know I was here, anyway?"

"I'm here because you got yourself into another damned mess, which means Ethan and I had to drop everything to drive up here to get you out of it." Cole ground out the words through clenched teeth.

"But how…"

Cole pulled his cell phone from his jeans pocket. He swiped the small screen and held it up. Lola watched as select video of her in Mayor's Court played out on the screen. The edited film included snippets of Jeb's and Officer Wilson's testimony, then skipped to the sexy kiss she'd shared with Dylan and ended with the mayor sentencing her to community service.

Before she could ask it, her brother answered the question rolling through her mind.

"And like most of the cell-phone videos people take of you, 'Lola Smacks the Law' is already an overnight sensation." He checked the screen. "Already over a million views on YouTube, not to mention other social-media sites."

"Oh, crap," Lola groaned. "Anyway, that's all wrong. I didn't hurt Officer Wilson. I was only helping—"

Cole held up a hand. "Save it. I've heard it all before. So has our entire family." As usual, his mind was already made up.

Ethan reached for another cinnamon roll. "Is that the reason you called yesterday?"

Lola nodded. "But that part is over. Officer Wilson lied, and no charges were filed against me."

Cole grunted. "Do you know how worried Sage, Tia and Dad have been? We've all left voice mail messages for you," he said, then added, "Messages you couldn't be bothered to answer."

"I'm sorry." Lola genuinely regretted having them worry needlessly. "My phone battery died, and I was so tired when I got here last night I totally forgot to charge it."

Then it occurred to her, if she'd missed her family's calls, had anyone else tried phoning after seeing the amateur video of her in Mayor's Court? Dread washed over as she thought about her agent. There was a strong possibility there might not be a job waiting on her, after all.

"It's always something with you, isn't it?" Cole glanced at his watch. "Get dressed and get your things together so we can hit the road. Ethan and I have already wasted enough time on your nonsense."

Nonsense.

It was one of the words her brother had used when they'd fired her. Now it rankled her even more.

"I can't leave Cooper's Place. You saw the video. My community service starts Monday morning," Lola said.

Cole dismissed her statement with a wave of his hand.

Ethan wiped icing off his fingertips with a napkin. "I've already talked to a lawyer friend here in

Ohio. He's waking up a judge as we speak to get him to sign an emergency stay on the contempt sentence. He's pretty sure he can get the entire thing tossed out on Monday."

Lola looked from her brother to her brother-in-law. She knew they meant well and had her best interest at heart. However, she couldn't help comparing their actions to Dylan's.

They'd come up with a solution to what they thought was a problem and had charged ahead. As usual, they hadn't bothered discussing it with her. Lola thought about the note Dylan had left on her suitcase. He'd come up with the same approach to attacking her dilemma, only he'd left any decisions to be made up to her.

The difference was respect.

Lola looked past her brother to Dylan, who was still leaning against the kitchen counter. He was wearing a different, more casual uniform this morning, khaki shorts and a white polo shirt with the police department's emblem on the chest pocket. Rock-solid, calm and confident, his quiet presence conveyed more than mere words ever could.

Their eyes met, confirming her conclusion: Dylan Cooper had her back.

"So are you going to get packed or do I have to go up there and do it for you?" Cole asked. "I've been driving all night, and I'm not in the mood for your ridiculousness this morning."

Ridiculousness.

Lola felt a prick of annoyance at the word, another

one they'd used yesterday. With her bare feet rooted
to the hardwood floor, she faced her older brother.
"I'm not going back to Nashville with you," she said,
and then turned briefly to Ethan. "And call off that
lawyer. I'll handle this my own way."

"Don't try me, Lola," Cole said.

The room went silent for a beat, and then she heard
Dylan clear his throat from across the room. "Usually, I don't stick my nose in a conversation between
family, but—"

"Then don't," Cole snapped, not bothering to look
at him.

"I'm afraid I can't do that." Dylan pushed off the
counter. Lola watched him walk across the kitchen
until he was beside her.

"Lola isn't going anywhere she doesn't want to go."

Dylan's tone wasn't combative. Neither was his
stance, although he towered over her brother and
brother-in-law, who each stood well over six feet tall.
Everything about him was cool and matter-of-fact.

Cole looked up at him. "Let's get something straight,
Hoss. This is my baby sister we're talking about, and
I'm not about to let some guy get in the way of my
doing what's best for her."

Dylan nodded. "I admire and understand the sen-
timent. In the short time I've known her, I've grown
to care about your sister, too," he said. "However,
I'm going to have to respectfully disagree with you
on a few points. First of all, Lola's no baby. She's an
adult who can decide for herself what's best for her."

Cole grunted at the words that made Lola's chest

expand with emotion for a man she'd known a single day. She couldn't explain it, but Dylan Cooper had managed to touch her heart in a way that made her feel as if he knew her better than anyone did.

Still, her brother wasn't having it. He chuckled, a humorless sound that reeked of sarcasm, and then glared at Dylan. "You claim to care about my sister, and you let her go through with that kangaroo court hearing last night."

"I didn't like it any more than you did. In fact, I advised Lola against going through with it."

Virginia topped off her and Ethan's coffee mugs. "Well, it seemed like a good idea at the time."

Cole kept his focus on Dylan. "Then why didn't you stop her, man?"

"Lola weighed her options and made up her own mind. It wasn't my place to stop her," Dylan said. "Only be there to support her decision."

"Even if the decisions she makes are dumb as hell?"

"Yes." Dylan's reply was directed to Cole, but his eyes shifted to her. "Even then."

Lola stared at him in shock. Had she really passed up a night in this man's bed?

The thought made her want to kick her own behind. In this particular case, her brother might have been right. Her decision not to go home with Dylan and experience those naughty things he'd whispered in her ear last night was indeed *dumb as hell*.

Cinnamon roll in hand, Ethan nudged Cole with his elbow. "Spoken like a man who's got his nose wide open by a pretty face and is willing to be led around by it," her brother-in-law said.

Cole grunted in agreement.

Dylan shrugged, not bothered by the comment. "There's no denying or ignoring Lola's beauty," he said. "However, anyone who's been lucky enough to see beyond her looks would also know she's wild, strong, independent and a little unpredictable. She's also one of the most compassionate people I've ever met, even when it's not easy." He smiled down at her. "Lola dives headfirst into life, and no matter how many knocks she takes along the way, her spirit is indestructible."

Wow. Lola stared up at him. Just wow.

Dylan Cooper didn't talk much. Nor did he toss around words casually. Lola wasn't certain what the ones he'd just spoken had melted faster—her heart or her panties. But she was pretty sure the latter would hit the floor the moment she had the man standing beside her alone.

Her brother, however, wasn't moved.

Cole threw his head back and laughed as if Dylan had told him the funniest joke he'd heard in years. Then, as if someone had flipped a switch, his tone grew serious. "Unlike my baby sister, who hasn't stopped making goo-goo eyes at you ever since she walked into this kitchen, I'm not fooled so easily," he said. "You expect us to believe you gleaned these things about her after knowing her, what?" he scoffed. "One day?"

Leave it to Cole to throw an ice bucket of logic in

her face. Or maybe this time she really was being ridiculous. No way could she be falling for Dylan this fast or this hard. *Could she?*

But logic once again flew out the window the moment Dylan reached for her hand. Lola couldn't explain it or even describe it; all she knew was, like the last pieces on a jigsaw puzzle, they fit, and what she felt was real.

"One day," Dylan confirmed. "A day from hell for your sister." He paused and really looked at her, and Lola knew those brown eyes she'd thought of as merely sexy yesterday could see into her very soul. "The kind of pressure she withstood yesterday reveals true character. The sheer frustration of it would have broken most people, but not Lola. Instead of being crushed, she sparkled like a diamond."

Cole, Ethan and Virginia looked on slack-jawed as he continued, and Lola found herself picking her chin off her chest, too.

"I wouldn't do a thing to try to temper or change her," Dylan said. "I want to hold her down—not hold her back."

Quiet fell over the kitchen. The man who didn't waste words had left them all scrambling to find theirs. For once, not even Cole had a retort.

"Well, damn," Virginia murmured, finally breaking the silence.

Cole looked at Lola, opened his mouth as if he were about to speak, and then closed it. When he opened it again, a long sigh escaped. "I guess you'll be okay here," he grumbled reluctantly. Then he turned to Dylan. "But if any harm comes to her while she's in this hick town, you being the police chief won't stop me and my brother-in-law from coming back here to kick your big, muscle-bound ass."

An hour, a second pot of coffee and a dozen cinnamon rolls later, Lola stood on the front porch of Virginia's house waving goodbye to her family. Both her brother and brother-in-law were eager to get back to Nashville and their wives, but vowed to return with Sage and Tia in tow if they got wind of any more trouble.

"What did you go and threaten him for?" Lola heard Ethan ask her brother as they got into Cole's black Dodge Challenger. "The two of us couldn't take that guy. Did you see that size of him?" Ethan emitted a low whistle. "That Dylan Cooper is one big..."

The car doors slammed shut, drowning out the rest of her brother-in-law's admonishment.

Lola continued to wave as the black muscle car roared down the street.

"I noticed you didn't mention the television gig to them," Dylan said.

Lola shrugged. "Even if I manage to get this community service delayed and make it to New York in time, I'm not sure that job is waiting on me anymore, especially with that Mayor's Court fiasco all over the web."

Once they were back inside, she retrieved her phone. Virginia was no longer in the kitchen, and Lola was grateful Dylan had lingered. She plugged the charger into an outlet to revive her phone and immediately began scrolling through the missed text messages. There were the concerned ones from her family, and again, she regretted making them worry. Then there were a bunch from her girlfriends, fishing for details on the hunk they'd seen her kissing in the video. She was relieved not to see Jill's number among them.

Lola swiped the screen to retrieve her voice mail messages and bit her lip. This time there was a message from Jill. Lola put the phone on Speaker. Dylan had worked hard to clear her name yesterday, as if he'd had as much vested in this opportunity as she had. It seemed right that he hear any update right along with her.

Unfortunately, the talent agent had said exactly what Lola had feared. The producers at *America Live!* had canceled her guest host stint on Monday.

"They were diplomatic about it, of course," Jill had said testily. "Their executive producer said she thought it best to postpone your appearance for a while, as in *indefinitely.*" Jill's long, put-upon sigh sounded from the tiny speaker, filling the cheery kitchen with its disapproval. "You couldn't even go twenty-four hours without landing yourself in the middle of another calamity."

The talent agent mentioned calling in some favors at the network to try to get her scheduled for another slot on the program. "But if I do that, I want you where I can keep an eye on you 24/7." Her voice was heavy with reproach.

Lola knew Jill was frustrated with her. Still, she

didn't appreciate her tone. And as with her brother earlier, Lola had no intention of trying to explain her actions.

She was done defending herself.

Jill ended the message with the same admonishment Lola had heard for what seemed her entire life. "Give me a call when you get this message. By then maybe I'll have come up with a strategy to fix your mess."

Fix her mess...

Lola glanced at Dylan. He didn't speak, but the frown on his face mirrored how she felt. She took the phone off Speaker and touched the screen to activate the callback function. Seconds later, Jill was ranting in her ear about blown opportunities and Lola being a magnet for trouble. Her agent hadn't even taken a breath to say hello or inquire how Lola was coping after yesterday's events.

"So what do you have to say for yourself now?"

A beat passed. One Lola would have once rushed to fill with explanations and a plea for understanding.

"Nothing," Lola said. "You're fired."

Ending the call, she met Dylan's gaze. A smile spread over his full lips. He held up his fist, and she promptly bumped it with her own.

"Good job," he said.

And Lola found that although she didn't need his approval to know she'd done the right thing, she liked having him in her corner.

"Does this mean you're free this weekend?" He lifted a brow.

"I have a list of appointments in New York to cancel." She began ticking them off on her fingers, including letting "Pablo" know he was free to enjoy his weekend. "Otherwise…"

In one swift movement, Dylan hauled her into his arms, and Lola gasped to catch her breath. He took full advantage of the opportunity her open mouth presented, and kissed her.

Lola's fingers clung to his broad shoulders as his tongue stroked hers, doing things to her mouth she longed for it to do to her entire body—over and over again. However, Dylan's kiss did more than stir her libido, more than make her desire him over any man. His taste, his clean masculine scent, the delicious feel of being in his strong embrace made her feel the same way their first kiss had, as if she'd been waiting for this her entire life.

When they finally came up for air, his dark brown eyes blazed into hers. "Do you remember how we planned to celebrate your victory in court? Well, before my uncle killed the mood."

Lola tapped her forefinger against his broad chest. "I spent the majority of last night regretting not going home with you."

"Well, there's an easy way to remedy that," he said.

"And does this remedy include you stripping?" Lola lifted a brow, feeling her panties dampen at the prospect.

"Definitely." The planes of his face softened as the corner of his mouth lifted. "But I won't dance."

His deep voice lowered an octave. "No matter how hard you spank me."

Lola slid her hand down and pinched his firm ass. "We'll see."

Dylan nuzzled her neck and she giggled.

"Hey, you two can save your kinky spanking fetish for the hospital waiting room. This isn't that kind of establishment."

They turned to find Virginia standing in the archway to the formal dining room. She peered around the kitchen.

"Did that bougie family of yours hit the road?"

Lola barely stifled a laugh. "Cole and Ethan headed back to Nashville a little while ago."

"Thank goodness. I thought I'd have to put up with that bossy brother of yours overnight." Virginia strode into her kitchen, visibly relieved. "If what I saw of him is any indication, I don't know how his poor wife puts up with him."

Lola thought of her brother and Sage, and this time she couldn't hold back her laughter. "Believe me, he and his wife are two of a kind," she assured the older woman.

Virginia glanced at her watch and then at her son. "Don't you have a patrol or something to get to?"

"I did a circuit around town and checked in at the station earlier." Dylan looked down at Lola, still wrapped in his embrace, as he continued to answer his mother's question. "But I do have two Little League games to umpire today, one this morning and another this afternoon. Maybe you can stop by the ballpark later?"

"Nope. She's busy today." Virginia answered for her. "So say goodbye, lover boy, because Lola and I have things to do."

"We do?" This was the first Lola had heard of it.

Once Dylan was out the door, Virginia surveyed her from head to toe and then tapped her biceps as if she were testing it. "So a scrawny thing like you was able to lift Wilson and drag him to your car all by yourself, huh?"

Chapter 12

Lola's brother-in-law had been right, Dylan thought that evening.

"Your nose is wide-open," he mumbled.

There was no other explanation.

After a scorcher of a day spent in the park umpiring two games, and then making his evening checks around town, the only thing on his mind should be diving into the cool, chlorinated waters of his backyard pool. Instead, thoughts of Lola consumed him as he drove home. Just as they had all day.

He couldn't wait to see her again.

Dylan had cleared his slate for the evening. He'd already checked in at the station, and then directed the county sheriff's department to handle any calls tonight. Now all that was left for him to do was shower, change clothes and then pick up Lola at his mom's. He'd planned to make dinner for her this evening. Green salad, and if the predicted rain held off, steaks on the grill. However, Dylan didn't rule out the possibility of her unearthing a packet of protein powder from her purse.

Like so many things about Lola, images of her and that huge pink purse she lugged around made him smile. In fact, Dylan thought he'd exercised his smile muscles more in the last twenty-four hours than he had in years.

He slowed the truck as he came upon his mother's house, and briefly debated whether to give in to his baser instinct. A part of him that wanted to kick in the door, throw Lola over his shoulder caveman-style and carry her to his truck.

Dylan vetoed the idea. The reality was anyone kicking in Virginia Cooper's front door would land himself on the wrong end of her shotgun. Also, a whiff of his shirt convinced him it would be better all around if he drove around the corner to his house for a shower, and then returned for Lola.

It was dusk when he parked in the carport attached to his ranch-style home. Dylan stuck his key in the side door leading into the house and froze. The concrete stones and sacks of concrete mix he'd stacked near the door yesterday morning were gone. They'd been here this morning when he'd left the house.

"What the..."

Then he heard the sound of splashing water coming from the backyard. Not only were the supplies for his mother's fire pit missing, someone was in his pool.

Back in Chicago, Dylan would have automatically reached for his service revolver before going inside his house to check things out. But this was Cooper's Place.

Instead, he slid a hand down his face and exhaled, as he summoned the patience that usually came naturally for him. Some teens on the block had probably moved the supplies as a prank, he reasoned. Now they were sneaking a dip in his pool after a blistering hot day.

He'd had a six-foot privacy fence erected around the backyard the day after the in-ground pool was installed. Still, the wall of pine was designed for solitude, not security. Dylan entered his house. Not bothering to turn on any lights, he stalked to the sliding glass doors leading to his backyard. Whoever had taken the liberty of trespassing was about to find out pool time was over, *now*.

After flinging open the door, Dylan charged across the stone patio. He felt a muscle tic along his jawline as he stood at the edge of the dimly lit pool watching the shadowy form slicing through the water near its bottom.

A svelte form that, as he continued to stare, revealed itself to be both female and very familiar.

"Lola." Dylan uttered the name just as her head popped up to the surface. The tension lodged between his shoulders receded, replaced by tension of an entirely different nature below his waist.

She blinked in surprise at the sight of him. Then that magnetic smile Dylan imagined sold millions of lipsticks to women desperate to achieve the same effect spread over her lips. It lit up her face, his backyard and his life.

Lola swam to the edge of the pool and folded her arms on the ledge near his feet. Water droplets clung to her heart-shaped face, shimmering like diamonds against her luminous skin. Her dark hair fell in wet waves down her back as she looked up at him.

"After working me like a dog all day, your mother offered me the use of your pool," she said by way of explanation.

Dylan smiled, thinking of the hours of labor his mother put into her flower garden. Like her kitchen, it was her pride and joy. She must have recruited Lola to help her with it, he thought.

"Mom can be a bit of a fanatic about her garden," he said. "Sorry you got drafted into pulling weeds all day."

"Garden?" Lola huffed. "You familiar with a program called *Granny's Old House*?"

Dylan's mind flashed to the items missing from the carport. "Are you saying you and my mom moved those supplies from my carport to her house?" Those concrete stones were heavy and that sack of mix weighed at least forty pounds. No way the two of them had done it. At least, not on their own.

"I moved them," Lola said. "Ginny supervised."

"Ginny?" Dylan gave his head a quick shake as if he hadn't heard her right. To his knowledge, no one, not even his dad, had ever called Virginia Cooper Ginny.

"She wasn't big on the nickname," Lola said, as if she'd read his mind. "But if I can spend all day laboring in the hot sun constructing her a backyard fire pit, I can most certainly call her Ginny."

"Y-you built that fire pit?" Dylan stammered, looking down at her in the water. He was no sexist, but he did have trouble reconciling the idea of his elderly mom and a woman who at most weighed a hundred and twenty pounds doing a job that even for him would have been backbreaking work.

"I did," she said proudly. "And the Granny who hosts that home-improvement show is full of it." Lola chuckled. "No way that job was 'as easy as arranging a vase of flowers'."

Dylan crouched down and smoothed the back of his hand down the side of Lola's face. Her wet skin felt like fine silk against his touch. "As with everything I've seen of you so far, Lola Gray, I'm impressed."

"Then you don't mind me using your pool?" She captured him with her gaze. Now Dylan was her prisoner, and he knew she could use anything she wanted of his, including him, for as long as she could stand it.

"Depends." He leaned lower and peered into the water. "Is that a red bikini you're wearing?"

Lola kissed him, and Dylan nearly lost his balance as his mouth melded with hers. Or was it his mind? Before he could decide or move to deepen the kiss, she abruptly broke it off and pushed off the pool's ledge. Dylan watched her disappear under the water, and when she reemerged a few seconds later her breasts were bare and her bikini top dangled from her outstretched hand.

He licked his lips at the sight of her pert, perfect breasts, feeling his cock grow harder than those concrete stones she'd hefted earlier.

"Actually, I'm only wearing half of a red bikini." She flung the top toward him, and Dylan caught the scrap of red in one large hand.

"You told me when we met that trouble was your middle name," he said. "Now I'm convinced you were right."

"Want to know what else I was right about?" The water rippled as her hands slid downward.

"What's that?" he asked.

She shimmied out of the bikini bottom and threw it in his direction. "I knew you'd melt the panties right off me."

Standing, Dylan snatched the miniscule garment from midair and tossed it over his shoulder. "Saves me the trouble of tearing them off your beautiful body." His voice lowered to a growl he barely recognized. *"With my teeth."*

Thunder rumbled in the distance as Dylan watched her swim to the pool's edge. He followed her gaze as it fell below his waist, where his arousal tented his increasingly uncomfortable pants.

"Well, damn." She looked up at his face briefly, before returning her attention to the *real* trouble her nakedness had stirred up. "Now it's my turn to be impressed."

His stiff cock twitched as if it was acknowledging the compliment. Dylan kicked off his shoes and unbuttoned his shirt. "So are you coming out of there, or do I have to come in and get you?"

"Come and get it," she demanded.

And Dylan didn't have to be told twice.

"Yes-s-s!"

Pinned between Dylan's solid body and a wall of glass, Lola found her hiss of pleasure filling the close confines of the shower. Her hands clutched the water-slicked skin of his wide shoulders and her open thighs wrapped around his waist as he buried himself inside her.

The evening skies had opened up seconds after Dylan dived into the pool. Still, not even the sudden downpour could cool the heated moment when their naked bodies made contact for the very first time.

It had taken a crack of lightning striking dangerously close to the pool to pull them apart, and then Dylan had scooped her up in his muscled arms and carried her into the house. Dripping wet, he'd carried her through to his bedroom, continuing past the king-size bed into the bath. Only then did he set her on her feet, but only long enough to pull her inside the shower with him under the warm spray.

And now he thrust inside her with a force that both rocked Lola's world and incited the fear they'd shatter the glass walls surrounding them. If the high notes she hit as she kept pace with him stroke for stroke didn't do it first.

Dylan eased off his unrelenting pace. His big body stilled, and he leaned in until his forehead rested against hers. Steam rose and the water rained down on them, dripping from the planes and angles of his face onto hers. Although the thrusts had slowed to a stop, his thick cock pulsed inside her, needy and insistent.

"You okay?" she asked.

"No," he rasped. "I'm supposed to be taking this slow and easy, savoring every touch, every kiss, every movement. I want to make our time together something neither of us can forget for a very long time."

With her legs still wrapped firmly around his waist, Lola lifted his chin with her fingertip until their gazes met. "Do you see me complaining?"

He appeared to think about it a moment, and then the corner of his sexy mouth lifted into a half smile. "No. I didn't."

Lola tightened her inner walls around his deeply embedded cock. "Does it feel like I don't like it?"

"God, no." Dylan's eyes slammed shut, and she could see him struggle for control.

"Slow and easy has its place, but I like it bumpy." Supported by both him and the wall, Lola slid her free hand down his broad back, past her legs around his waist, and pinched his fine ass. "Don't worry about me, Chief. I can handle the ride."

Chapter 13

Dylan rolled over and looked at Lola, who'd just collapsed onto the other side of his bed with a satisfied sigh.

"Thought you could handle a bumpy ride?" He crooked his elbow and rested his head in the palm of his hand. Dawn had leaked through the narrow slats of the window blinds, illuminating the room in soft light. He watched the rise and fall of Lola's breasts with his own sense of satisfaction as she caught her breath.

"Oh, my gawd, that was good," she managed to sigh between pants.

"I heard." Dylan felt the corner of his mouth lift. "In fact, I think everyone on my street heard you."

"Oh, no." Lola grabbed the sheet and snatched it

over her head. She pulled it back just enough to reveal her face. Her teeth studied her bottom lip, which was already puffy from a night of his nonstop kisses. "Was I that loud?"

Dylan thought of the last ride she'd taken—on his face—and his half smile broadened to a full-on grin. "Fortunately, your thighs covered my ears and muffled the screams."

"Egomaniac, much?" Lola rolled her eyes.

Dylan rolled onto his back and pulled her into his arms. "I guess a night of being told how remarkable I am, over and over again, went to my head."

"Next time, I'm going to see to it you're the one doing the shouting, even if I have to…" She whispered the rest in his ear, and Dylan's cock stirred beneath the sheet.

Lola didn't miss it. "Damn," she mumbled. "How did your ex ever walk away from that…uh, I mean you…"

Dylan laughed, loud and hard. He tapped the tip of her nose with his finger. "You really do say exactly what's on your mind, don't you?"

The quirkiness and unabashed honesty of the woman beside brought out another side of him. A version that smiled often and enjoyed a good laugh.

Dylan had tried to resist Lola, especially when she was under suspicion. But those facets of her nature, more than her incredible beauty, had gotten under his skin and made a place for her in his heart.

She lifted her head and rested her chin on his chest. "I do," she confirmed. "And for the life of me, I can't imagine…" Her voice trailed off. "Sorry, I shouldn't be so nosy."

"I think it's a side effect of you being trapped in Cooper's Place. Everyone here is nosy." He caressed her cheek. His ex had left for the same reason Lola would in a few days.

Despite its foibles, Dylan counted returning to his hometown as one of the best decisions he'd ever made. However, a town this size was too small for his ex to live her dreams, and it was too small to hold on to someone with Lola's exuberant personality.

Sure, she'd had some tough luck careerwise this week, but it wouldn't be long before the people who'd rejected her would see the error of their ways or even better offers would come along. "My marriage broke up for the same reasons a lot of them do," Dylan said aloud. "We got married too young, before we figured out what we really wanted in life. By the time we did, we both wanted different things more than each other."

"That's sad," Lola said.

Dylan felt a small ache, but it had nothing to do with his past. He and Lola were on the clock, and in a few days she'd be gone. He didn't want to waste one precious second.

"It was also a long time ago, and the furthest thing from my mind with you in my bed." Dylan shifted until she was on top of him.

Threading his fingers through her hair, he brushed his lips against hers in the gentlest kiss a man his size could manage.

She closed her eyes and sighed against his mouth. "God, I l-lo—" She abruptly stopped midword, and her eyes snapped open. "I really like you, Dylan Cooper." She bit her lip. "I like you a lot."

Dylan swallowed. "I like you, too, Lola," he said. *So very much*, he thought.

Their words belied the truth they saw in each other's eyes. Lola chuckled, but it sounded awkward to both of them.

"Anything more would be crazy, right?" she asked. "I mean, who falls in love in two days?"

Dylan didn't answer her last question, at least not aloud. The reality was it had been a rhetorical one. Deep down, they both knew who'd found love so quickly. Regardless of how crazy it felt.

They had.

Lola squirmed on top of him, and his groin tightened, eager to show her what he hadn't been ready to tell her.

Later that morning, Dylan set a steamy mug of coffee on the bedside table near a dozing Lola. She sniffed the air, yawned and stretched her arms over her head.

"Morning," she croaked groggily. She cracked open her eyes and blinked. "You're already dressed?"

Lola pushed herself up on her elbows and ran a hand through her hair. "When did you get up? What time is it?"

"It's after ten," Dylan said.

"Ten?" She glanced at the clock on his side of the

bed for confirmation. "I never sleep this late. Then again, I've been on a ride that lasted all night long."

Bombarded by images of the night before, Dylan smiled. "It's why I slipped out without disturbing you. I figured you needed your rest and coffee."

Lola wrapped the porcelain mug in her hands, brought it to her nose and inhaled deeply. "You've already been out?"

Dylan nodded. "I did my early-morning patrol, checked in at the station and with the sheriff's office to see if they'd had any calls from Cooper's Place last night." He raised a brow. "Fortunately, nobody reported a woman screaming my name all night long."

She raised a brow in turn. "Well, there's always tonight."

"And the rest of the morning, this afternoon and…"

"I like the sound of that." She took a sip of coffee. "But first I need to get my purse off your patio and mix up some breakfast. I'm starved."

"I already brought your purse inside. It's in the kitchen, along with a batch of blueberry muffins I picked up from my mom's," he said. "They should still be warm."

"Muffins!" Lola threw back the covers, revealing her gloriously naked body. A form he'd explored every inch of with his hands and his tongue.

Dylan pulled her into his arms. "So don't you think I deserve a morning kiss?"

Lola smoothed a fingertip over his lips. "But you already kissed me good-morning, *everywhere*."

Ten minutes later, Dylan was in the kitchen pouring himself a cup of coffee when Lola appeared, shower fresh and wrapped in his robe. She seated herself on one of the stools at his breakfast bar.

"I hope you don't mind my borrowing this," she said. "All I have is my bikini and the sarong I wore over here yesterday."

"Actually, I'm the one guilty of being presumptuous, again." He glanced down at the plates and basket of muffins on the breakfast bar's granite surface, and then back to her. "I knew you didn't have any clothes, so I brought your suitcase over."

Lola dismissed his concern with a wave of her hand and then immediately pulled back the cloth covering the muffins and grabbed one. "That's fine by me. In fact, I appreciate it. You saved me from doing a one-night-stand walk of shame back to the B and B wearing the same clothes, well, bikini, I had on yesterday." She spread a pat of butter over the muffin. "I can just imagine the rumors that would cause around here, and I wouldn't want to ruin your reputation."

He watched her take a huge bite of the muffin. She closed her eyes as she slowly chewed.

"I think you did that five minutes after we met in the hospital waiting room." Dylan shrugged. "Everyone in town already believes I can't keep my clothes on around you, and last night, I proved those rumors to be true."

"I like you without clothes." Lola winked.

Right now, Dylan wished he had Lola's gift of unabashed openness. "But I didn't bring your things here just so you'd have something to change into," he hedged. "I'm sure you're going to want to hightail it out of here as soon as you complete that ridiculous community service sentence, and I don't blame you. Still, I was hoping as long as you're in town, you might like to stay here, with me."

Dylan felt as awkward as a teenager asking out a girl who was out of his league. He looked across the kitchen island counter at the stunning face she was currently stuffing with a second blueberry muffin.

Hell, Lola Gray is *out of your league.*

She licked a crumb from her fingertip and hopped off the stool. She rounded the counter, threw her arms around his neck and kissed him.

"I can't think of anything I'd like more than riding out my time here with you," she said.

Dylan wrapped one arm around her slim waist and pulled her to him until her slight curves melded against him. "It's only fair I warn you it could get bumpy," he said, so she knew he'd caught her meaning.

Her arms slipped from around his neck until her hands rested on his shoulders, taking Dylan back to making love to her in the shower.

"Then I'll just have to hang on tight, while I enjoy the ride."

They were down to one last muffin when Dylan poured them each a second cup of coffee, and Lola was eyeballing it.

"What about those shake packets in your purse?" He sat on the vacant stool next to her at the breakfast bar.

Lola snatched the last muffin from the basket. "I've not only been fired from my job, I was let go from one I hadn't even started," she said. "So today, I'll eat whatever I please. Maybe tomorrow, too, I'll need my strength to get through those community-service hours."

Tension settled in Dylan's shoulders as he thought about that fiasco of a hearing in Mayor's Court, and what he'd heard this morning of his uncle's plans for Lola to fulfill her sentence. Dylan knew how rumors stretched the limits of incredulousness, especially in Cooper's Place, but he was pretty sure this one held more than a kernel of truth.

"Keep in mind, I'm not trying to second-guess your decision, but…"

"Too late." Lola polished off the last of the muffin.

Dylan smiled and then shook his head. "Are you positive you don't want either your brother-in-law or my attorney friend to get you out of this community service nonsense?" he asked. "I doubt what Uncle Roy did was even legal, and it could be easily dismissed."

"It's only a couple of hours. Besides, I do my best thinking when I'm working, so it'll give me time to figure out my next career move."

She swiveled the stool he was sitting on until his back was to her, and then she began to massage his stiff shoulders with her fingertips. "Relax, Dylan. It'll be fine."

"But you don't understand." Dylan took a moment to fill her in. "He'd initially planned to have you pick-ing up litter along Main Street. However, after Rosemary Moody stopped by Mom's yesterday and saw the fire pit you built…"

"Rosemary would be the one who thought I did denture adhesive commercials, right?" Lola continued to knead his shoulders.

"That would be her," Dylan said. "And by the way, I saw the fire pit this morning, I don't think I could have done a better job."

"Thanks, but I still don't get how my building it affects my community-service sentence."

"My uncle wants his next inauguration to be held in the town square, and he's been banging the drum to reallocate the town's budget to have it spruced up." Dylan could see where the white picket fence surrounding the square could use a fresh coat of paint. The gazebo, too. "Anyway, the public works department has the supplies, but labor has been the sticking point. The town can't afford the overtime."

Lola's fingers stopped working their relaxing magic. "Ah, I get it now. I'll be supplying the labor tomorrow."

"Now do you understand my concern?" Dylan looked over his shoulder at her. "He's one of the reasons you lost that opportunity to guest host *America Live!* It's not fair that you end up painting the very gazebo he takes his next oath of office in."

Lola scrunched up her nose in concentration. "Has he even been reelected yet?"

Dylan shook his head. "But he always runs unopposed, so it's pretty much a forgone conclusion."

She snorted and resumed rubbing his shoulders.

"What this place needs is a new mayor," she said. "I know he's your family and all, but Roy Cooper is an…"

"Ass." They said the word simultaneously and broke into laughter.

Dylan turned around in the chair and took her hands in his. "So you see why I'm uncomfortable with this community-services business?"

"I'm a big girl, Dylan. I can fix my own messes."

"I know you can." He gently squeezed her hands. "But I'm an even bigger man, who in a short period of time has grown to *like you very much*." Dylan paused to let her absorb his real meaning, before exhaling. "However, it's your decision to make, and I'll stand by it."

He brought her hands to his lips and kissed them.

"Thank you." She slid off the stool.

"Now get dressed." Dylan stood. "I'm going to have the sheriff's office cover any calls today, so we can spend it together. I want to show you more of Cooper's Place than my mother's backyard and Marjorie's pink jail cell."

"Perhaps we can persuade Ginny to make another lemonade layer cake and maybe more of that buttermilk fried chicken you, she and Marjorie practically inhaled right in front of me the other night," Lola said.

"That won't be a problem. She's already insisted on you coming for Sunday dinner," Dylan stated. "She also said for you not to bring any protein-mix packets or talk of cockamamie diets at her table."

Lola giggled. "I'm not going to even think about my diet, until I leave town."

The smile on her face dimmed. It reflected how Dylan felt inside. "Let's just focus on enjoying today and getting your community service done tomorrow." He grabbed his cell phone off the kitchen island. "I'm going to call the sheriff's office dispatcher, while you get dressed."

"Oh, you might also want to ask them for some assistance with the media tomorrow," she said.

"Media?"

She nodded, and then walked to the corner of the kitchen where he'd left her suitcase. "Cell-phone videos of your uncle sentencing me to community service are all over the internet. Like it or not, the media will be here tomorrow morning," she said. "Joe Schmoe doing a menial task to serve a community service sentence is no big deal, but the latest Lola Gray fiasco will be a media event." She snorted. "Luckily, I don't have a job to get fired from this time."

Lola rolled the suitcase past him on her way to the bedroom. Dylan reached out to stop her.

"Any job where you'd have to temper the wild, impulsive and marvelously over-the-top side of your personality isn't worthy of you."

"But those are the very things that tend to get me in trouble," she said.

Dylan shook his head. "No. Those are the things, even more than your incredible beauty, that make you truly remarkable."

Chapter 14

Lola managed to elude the media Monday morning. However, she knew the reprieve was just temporary. The television crews would remain camped out at the entrance of the town's public works building for only so long, awaiting her community service walk of shame. Eventually, they'd get tipped off or catch on that she was actually a few streets away in the town square and had begun serving her sentence over an hour ago.

Removing the pink baseball cap from her head, she swiped at the sweat on her face with her forearm and took a step back to inspect her work. The overhead sun beamed down on her. It also revealed spots on the gazebo's latticework she'd missed with her paintbrush.

She bent over to dip the brush into the pail of white paint, but stopped when she saw a large shadow on the grass. A shiver of pure delight shimmied through her. Only one man could cast that big of a shadow.

"You don't have to keep checking on me." She looked over her shoulder. Sure enough, he was standing behind her in uniform, aviator shades shielding his eyes from the sun. "I'm fine."

"Who says I'm here checking on you?" Dylan asked. "It could be I just like looking at a pair of long legs in sexy cutoff shorts."

He sidled up to her and gave her a bottle of cold water. Lola sent him a grateful smile as she twisted off the cap and took a long swig.

"I would have thought you'd seen enough of my legs over the weekend," she said.

"Barely saw them at all, considering they were either hugging my waist or draped over my back," he said. "But I'm not complaining." He nudged her side with his elbow. "I didn't hear you complaining, either."

Their weekend together, though low-key, had been amazing both in and out of bed, Lola thought. Her work as the face of Espresso had afforded her the privilege of being fawned over in the most exciting cities in the world on nearly every continent. However, those places couldn't compare to the day she'd spent with Dylan, seeing another side of Cooper's Place, or the two incredible nights she'd spent in his arms.

Lola smiled up at him. "I was too well fed to do any complaining."

Not only had Ginny prepared the buttermilk fried chicken Lola had requested, she'd made a wide array of irresistible side dishes, and both her lemonade layer cake and a blueberry cobbler for dessert.

"No kidding." Dylan chuckled. "You dived face-first into that cobbler and ate it faster than the winner in a pie-eating contest."

His comment caught Lola off guard, and the gulp of water she'd just taken spewed right back out of her mouth. "I—I wasn't that bad," she sputtered.

Dylan looked down at her mouth. "Your lips are still blue."

"Well, there was plenty of lemonade cake for everyone else." Lola sniffed.

There had also been plenty of people there, she thought, still taken aback that Ginny's simple Sunday dinner had been more of an impromptu welcome party. Half the town had been there. Lola had recognized many of them from when they'd crowded into the police side of the public safety building to get a look at her, and she'd seen others in Mayor's Court.

However, unlike those sightings, she'd gotten to know them yesterday, both over dinner and earlier, when Dylan had showed her around town. Avis, the nurse from the hospital, was also the best pitcher on the medical facility's softball team and largely responsible for them winning a first-place intramural trophy two seasons in a row. Tammy, the waitress from the diner, was writing a mystery novel. An Ohio transplant originally from Florida, Jeb was bilingual and spoke fluent Spanish.

"You got quiet all of a sudden. Something wrong?" Dylan asked.

Lola shook her head. "I was just thinking about some of the conversations I had at your mother's house yesterday."

"I saw you talking to Jeb, and you both were all smiles. Did he apologize for accusing you of attacking Wilson?"

"No," Lola said. "Actually, with his bad eyesight, I don't think he ever realized who he was talking to."

"Probably not," Dylan said.

"But seriously, I had a great time. The people here are really amazing."

Dylan's eyes rounded. "I'm surprised you can say that after everything we put you through," he said. "This town's gossip mill is probably the reason you're not sitting in the guest host's seat on *America Live!* right now."

She shrugged. "It was an accumulation of things, so if anyone is to blame, it's me for always getting into jams." Lola had thought about it last night. The words of the man standing next to her had come to mind then, as they did now. She rested her fingertips on his muscled biceps. "But any job I have to temper myself to get isn't worthy of me."

Dylan wrapped an arm around her and pulled her closer to his side. He didn't say anything, but words weren't necessary. The smile he graced her with said it all. In a world where she was often misunderstood, Dylan Cooper got her, and right now, that was all that mattered.

"Speaking of jobs…" Dylan finally spoke. "You're doing a good one on this gazebo."

"Thanks. And I appreciate your having the public-works manager meet me here with the supplies rather than my having to face that throng of media." Although Lola knew he'd merely bought her a little time, it had been nice to be able to get lost in a project that allowed her mind to drift, so she could forget her problems.

Dylan continued to stare at the gazebo. "First the fire pit, now painting. You've got some pretty decent do-it-yourself skills."

"When I was growing up, my parents were consumed with Espresso business, which left me at home with a nanny and the household staff. They figured out early that putting me to work helping them with minor jobs kept me out of trouble and their hair." Lola looked at the gazebo. She was only halfway through the job. Still, it was gratifying how much a little paint had breathed new life into the weather-beaten structure. "I guess I am doing a good job on it," she said.

Dylan frowned. "Only for my uncle to take his oath of office underneath it after the next election."

As if on cue, a breeze rustled the trees. It blew a campaign placard that had been stapled to an oak off the tree and sent it tumbling through the grass, to land at Lola's feet. Dylan picked it up, and they both looked at the red letters emblazoned across it, imploring citizens to vote Roy Cooper mayor.

"Ass." The word tumbled out of their mouths at the exact same time, and they grinned at each other.

For a candidate running unopposed, Roy Cooper certainly had plenty of campaign material posted all over town, Lola thought.

She polished off the bottle of water, then tossed the empty in a nearby bin marked for plastic recyclables, and the campaign placard in the one designated for paper.

She looked up to see reporters at the far end of the square, and the smile dropped from her lips. "Damn."

Dylan followed her gaze. "Do you want to talk to them?"

Lola was no stranger to the media. She'd talked to plenty of reporters during her long stint as the face of her family's business. She'd also spent plenty of time defending herself to both them and people who'd already made up their minds about her.

The beauty of being between careers now was she didn't owe the media or anyone else any explanations for her behavior. "Not really, but I won't run and hide, either," she said. "I'll handle them."

"She's over there by the gazebo."

Dylan picked up the paint bucket and the brush Lola had been using. He held them out to her. "Take these and finish painting the gazebo."

"I already told you, Dylan. I'm a big girl, and I can handle my own messes."

"I know you can, but safeguarding you is more than my personal duty. It's my job," he said. "This is public property, and I can't keep them out of the square. However, I can make sure they don't invade your personal space."

Lola took the proffered paint and brush. She didn't even turn around to look at the descending cameras and microphones. Dylan had said he'd handle them, and Lola was confident this man could handle anything.

Minutes later she heard the furious clicks of cameras, flashbulbs and reporters calling out her name with the familiarity of long lost friends. Lola ignored them. Usually, that wouldn't have been possible, and she'd be swarmed with cameras and microphones mere inches from her face.

"Lola! Are they going to have you picking up trash or scrubbing toilets as part of your sentence?" one of them called out in an attempt to bait her.

"Can we get some photos of you without the baseball cap?" another female photographer yelled.

Lola ignored them, and continued to focus her attention on painting the gazebo's intricate latticework. She didn't look up until a few of them apparently tried to rush the gazebo and ran into a wall.

A well-over-six-foot wall made of solid muscle.

"Hey! It's not against the law for us to get close to her. You can't stop us," a man holding a microphone said.

But Dylan did stop them with his solid, unyielding presence, and he didn't have to utter a single word.

More people began to gather, leaving their various shops on the streets surrounding the town square to see what the commotion was all about. Lola recognized them from both the police station and Mayor's Court, but thanks to Ginny's dinner party she could not only put names with faces, she knew a lot of their stories.

Gary was among them, wearing another Hawaiian-print shirt, along with Dylan's former teacher, Mrs. Bartlett, who had filled Lola in on Dylan's school days.

They all stood by Dylan and the two sheriff's deputies who were keeping the media at a distance.

"What's going on here?" a reporter yelled.

"Yeah, we want to talk to Lola!" another one called.

"Well, Lola's not interested in talking to you," a woman said.

Lola and nearly everyone else turned to stare. It was Rosemary Moody.

The reporters continued with their questions. "Hey, Lola! Where's that cop you beat up? Still in the hospital?"

Lola sighed. She hadn't planned on answering any questions, but the damaging rumors of her being violent were really too much to let go. She dropped the paintbrush back into the pail. Before she could open her mouth to protest, another voice sounded out on the matter.

"Lola never beat up or hurt anyone. It was a misunderstanding," Tammy said.

"She dragged young Wilson to the hospital for help," a woman Lola recognized as the emergency-room receptionist said. "And she refused to leave until she knew he was okay. If anything, Lola is a Good Samaritan."

"Besides, that matter was all sorted out," Mrs. Bartlett added.

Lola's mouth remained open, this time in astonishment. Not only were the people from this sleepy little town defending her, they, along with Dylan, had formed a human barrier between her and the media.

"Over here, Lola!" a reporter from one of the tabloid television shows yelled. "Is it true *America Live!* canceled a guest host spot you were scheduled to do today because you can't stay out of trouble?"

"I know you!" The sunlight hit Gary's faded Born to Raise Hell tattoo as he raised his arm and pointed a finger at the reporter. "You're the anchor who got fired from the network for soliciting a prostitute." Gary let out a low whistle and shook his head. "Man, I wouldn't have wanted to be in your shoes. Must have been tough to explain to the wife how you lost a six-figure job 'cause you tried to pay for a piece of—"

"Gary Henson!" Mrs. Bartlett scolded.

"Sorry, Mrs. Bartlett." Like everyone else in town, Lola noticed, Gary's voice immediately adopted the singsong quality of a fifth-grader when he responded to the teacher's admonishment.

The reporters tossed out a few more questions, all designed to either provoke or embarrass her, but each time, a citizen of Cooper's Place either answered it or shouted it down. They'd known her for only a few days, yet she felt like one of their own. Lola couldn't remember ever feeling so incredibly touched, and it nearly brought her to tears. She willed the ones in her eyes not to fall. There were dozens of cameras

aimed in her direction, and the last thing she wanted
was a show of emotion on her part to be taken out
of context.

"There's no news story here." A familiar voice
came from the crowd of townspeople, and Lola spotted Dylan's mother in the throng. "Go back to where
you came from."

The crowd grumbled nosily in agreement.

Lola exhaled when it appeared some of the reporters were packing up to leave. However, her relief was
short-lived.

"Lola!" one of them shouted out. Lola recognized
the petite pixie of a woman instantly. This wasn't a
reporter from one of the news networks or celebrity-
stalking tabloid shows. Willow Gates, also known
as the Wicked Glam Mother, ran a popular blog on
the beauty industry, and her YouTube channel now
boasted over seven million followers.

"Is it true you're being replaced as the face of
Espresso Cosmetics by a drag queen?" the Wicked
Glam Mother asked. "By your very own brother?"

Lola flinched. The blogger's question had the effect of ripping a newly formed scab off a wound, and
Lola swallowed hard. A hush fell over the crowd. She
waited a beat before attempting to answer, because
this question required one and it had to come straight
from her mouth.

Dylan, who had been facing the crowd, turned to
look at her. He removed his aviator shades and those
mesmerizing brown eyes locked on her. He was a
man of few words, but his expression and solid pres-

ence told her everything she needed to know. Then the words he'd spoken in Ginny's kitchen echoed in her head, and she knew that was when she'd fallen in love with Dylan Cooper.

I want to hold her down—not hold her back.

Lola had believed him then and did even more so now. All she had to do was blink, and Dylan would clear this entire square for her. However, Lola didn't need him to. His being here was enough.

Now it was time for her to handle her business.

"Don't be so nosy," Rosemary Moody admonished the popular blogger, which set off a ripple of raised eyebrows throughout the crowd of Cooper's Place residents. "That's between Lola and her family," the town gossip added.

Family.

The very people Lola had basically told to kiss her ass on the way out of the Espresso building had jumped in a car and driven all night because they believed she needed their help. Cole could be obnoxious, and more than a touch overbearing, but he was also generous, protective, a loving brother and a good businessman.

Lola cleared her throat. "Yes, it's true that I will no longer be the face of Espresso Cosmetics," she said, finally replying to the question.

However, it apparently wasn't enough of an answer to satisfy the Wicked Glam Mother. "Don't you find it humiliating that a model of your stature was fired by her very own brother, and to add insult to injury, replaced by a man in drag?"

The woman had the word *wicked* in her name for a reason, Lola thought. Reporters and cameramen who had initially started packing up their equipment to leave stood riveted, awaiting Lola's answer. Their microphones and cameras were poised to capture every word.

Lola glanced at Dylan. His aviator sunglasses were back in place, but she saw the corner of his mouth twitch upward in the hint of a smile. The tiny gesture infused her with the cool confidence that came so naturally to him.

"I won't lie to you, Willow. I was taken aback by the decision," she began. "However, my brother is CEO of Espresso Cosmetics, and I know he'll do what's best for the company founded by our late mother."

"But *Lola.*" The blogger stretched out the two syllables of her name. "Aren't you embarrassed? Isn't your pride the tiniest bit bruised?"

Lola zeroed in on the woman as cameras clicked in the background. "Regardless of whether I'm Espresso's model, I'm still a part owner of that company. Like the rest of my family, my primary concerns are profits and preserving the legacy of Selena Sinclair Gray, not my ego."

Fifteen minutes later, only Dylan lingered. The town's citizens had returned to their daily routines, and the national media had abandoned the square. They'd quickly jumped into their various vehicles and exited town to pursue their next stories.

Lola exhaled. She was officially old news.

She turned to Dylan. "I appreciate you not intervening."

"There was no need. You handled it, and I couldn't be prouder."

"You seem distracted. You okay?" Lola asked.

"Sure. I was thinking when you finish your community-service hours, and I knock off work for the evening, we could celebrate with milkshakes at the diner," Dylan said. "We can celebrate you completing your sentence and getting the media off your back."

"I'd love that."

Lola leaned in and kissed him, being careful not to get any paint on his uniform. She couldn't see his eyes in the mirror of his wire-rimmed shades, but again she got the feeling something was wrong. She brushed it off as paranoia. Apparently she'd grown so used to things going wrong, she wasn't accustomed to them going right.

Dylan looked at the gazebo and then the grass. "I can give you a hand with that," he offered. "Marjorie will contact me if there are any calls."

Lola shook her head. "I appreciate the offer, but I'd rather do it myself," she said. "It'll give me time to figure out my next career move."

Hours after Dylan left the square, Lola put the finishing touches on the gazebo and stood back to admire it. She'd completed her required community service time over an hour ago, but wanted to finish the project she'd started.

"Looks good, Ms. Gray. I can hardly wait for inauguration day."

Lola spared a glance at Mayor Roy Cooper, and then busied herself gathering up the unused paint and supplies to return to the town's public works department. For once, she resisted the impulse to say what she was thinking, and the overwhelming urge to call Dylan's uncle an ass.

Chapter 15

"I already told you, I'm not sleepy."

Lola's protests would have carried more weight with Dylan if her eyes hadn't drifted shut and her head hadn't lolled until her chin touched her chest.

After dinner, he'd taken her to the movie playing this week at the town's lone theatre, where he quickly discovered her impulsive streak extended to yelling out advice to the characters on the big screen. Surprisingly, no one had complained.

Cooper's Place had quickly adopted her as one of their own. Like Dylan, they'd chalked up the outbursts to another case of Lola being Lola, and there was absolutely nothing wrong with that.

He moved to pry the television remote from her hand so he could switch off the fifty-inch flat screen mounted to his living room wall. Then he planned to scoop her off the sofa and carry her to bed.

Her eyes popped open. "No, I want to stay up and watch the show," she said, still battling with sleep.

"You're clearly exhausted," Dylan said. "How about I record it? We can watch it together in the morning."

"It's not the same." Her eyes closed again, but she kept a death grip on the remote. Tucking her bare feet under her, she snuggled against him, utilizing his chest as a pillow. "I'm just going to rest my eyes for a few minutes, but I'm not going to sleep."

The gentle snores that came out of her mouth seconds later indicated otherwise.

Dylan wrapped an arm around her. "Okay, you win. I'll wake you up when it comes on," he whispered, taking in her sleeping face.

Awake, there were so many fascinating facets to the woman seated next to him. Her warmth, openness, sense of humor and impulsiveness were so compelling, they made him nearly forget her exceptional beauty. He studied her sleeping face, committing it to memory. Because it wouldn't be long before she and what they had was just that—a memory.

Dylan glanced up at the television. She even had him tuning in to the Fashion Channel on a TV that up until now showed only games and sports highlights. Lola had received an email on her phone earlier that the blogger who had asked all those nosy questions in the square had a segment on Lola airing on the network's top show, *Beauty Outtakes*, tonight.

Lola had been nervous about it throughout their meal, after she'd read it. She'd explained how both the blogger and the show were widely followed by consumers and the cosmetics industry, and were very influential.

Dylan had felt anxious, too, albeit for selfish reasons.

He'd seen her in action. She'd done a spectacular job handling that blogger's intrusive inquiries on what he knew had to still be a sensitive subject for Lola. Dylan also had a strong feeling that once the blogger's segment and other news footage aired of a poised, eloquent and beautiful Lola, she'd charm viewers, just as she had him. The job offers would come rolling in.

It was only a matter of time. He'd realized that today at the town square. He'd also realized saying goodbye to her would be one of the hardest things he'd ever done in his life.

Dylan looked up at the television, where a woman was going on about a pair of needle-heeled pumps as if she was teaching a university course on them. The woman dangled a shoe from her finger. "Be sure to tune in next week for another riveting episode of *The Shoe Professor...*"

Dylan grunted and made another try for the remote. This time he managed to slip it out of Lola's hand without disturbing her.

He'd aimed it at the television with the intention of muting the volume, when video footage of Lola from this afternoon appeared on the screen.

"Next on *Beauty Outtakes* special correspondent Willow Gates, also know as the Wicked Glam Mother, gets misbehaving diva Lola Gray's reaction to her ousting as the face of Espresso Cosmetics."

Dylan turned up the television and gently shook Lola. "Wake up, sweetheart, the show's about to start." He wasn't the kind of guy who used endearments, but this one came as naturally to him as breathing.

Lola's eyelids fluttered, and she muttered something unintelligible, but otherwise didn't respond to his attempts to rouse her from sleep. Dylan dropped a kiss on her forehead and pressed the record button on the remote.

Then he watched the woman sleeping in his arms light up the television as her afternoon with the media replayed on the screen. Her casual appearance—cutoff denim shorts and dark hair tucked beneath a cap—didn't dim the wattage of her star power, Dylan observed. Lola Gray possessed the illusive It factor, along with a new confidence that she'd seemed to develop over the past few days.

The segment ended with the Wicked Glam Mother giving her impression of Lola to the host of *Beauty Outtakes*.

"I'd met Lola's sister-in-law, Sage Sinclair, last Valentine's Day. However, this was my first encounter with the infamous Lola Gray, and after all the media reports about her, I wasn't sure what to expect."

The blonde host of the show tilted her head toward the blogger conspiratorially. "Same here. I was actually holding my breath when I watched the footage of you asking her about being fired from her own company."

The pixyish blogger placed a hand to her chest. "So was I."

"Then you just wouldn't let up with those questions about how humiliating it must have been to be replaced by a drag queen." The host shook her head.

The blogger winked. "Honey, they don't call me 'wicked' for nothing."

Dylan frowned at the screen, remembering how difficult it had been for him to stand down and not clear the entire square of media. But there had been too many well-meaning people in Lola's life, constantly telling her what was best for her and bulldozing over her wishes.

Dylan instinctively knew Lola didn't need his advice or protection. What she needed, what she craved, was his respect, and that's exactly what he'd given her, because she'd earned it.

The pixie and the host of *Beauty Outtakes* continued their chatter.

"I swear I thought she was going to throw that bucket of white paint on you," the host said.

"So did I, but she surprised me," the blogger replied. "I think she shocked a lot of people, who were expecting a temper tantrum—or one of her infamous beat downs. However, she wasn't like that at all. I think Lola handled herself exceptionally well. I also believe a lot of the stories surrounding her lately are just that—innuendo and made-up stories."

The show's host chimed in. "I think letting an eloquent beauty like Lola go is Espresso's loss, and my sources tell me the producers at *America Live!* regret canceling her rumored guest-host spot, too," the blonde said.

"Lola's not only stunningly beautiful, she managed to rally an entire town around her without lifting a finger. I don't think she'll have trouble finding work," the Wicked Glam Mother said.

Dylan watched as the blonde nudged the blogger and lowered her voice to a staged whisper.

"In fact, you and our viewers at home didn't hear this from me, but there's been some water cooler talk in the Fashion Channel offices about the possibility of her being tapped to do a show on our network."

The segment ended, and Dylan stopped the recording and turned off the television. He sat motionless on the sofa, taking what he expected would be one of his last opportunities to savor the feel of Lola against him and the gentle weight of her head resting on his chest.

He glanced around his modest home, located on a tree-lined street in a small town. He loved it here and being surrounded by friends and family. It was enough for him, but it could never be enough for the woman in his arms.

The tiny flashing lights of Lola's silenced cell phone, resting on the end table, caught Dylan's eye. Her phone was blowing up already, he thought. Just as he'd predicted, the world had discovered the delightful attributes he'd seen in Lola Gray all along.

Now he'd have to do something that would be more difficult than not intervening when the media had descended on her today—let her go. It would be one of the hardest things he'd ever done in his life, because without a doubt he liked Lola Gray. He liked her so damn much.

"It's a wonderful opportunity and an extremely generous offer, but I'll need time to think it over. I'll get back to you in a few days with my decision."

Lola ended the call, unable to decide whether to hug or pinch herself. Last night, she'd fallen asleep with no employment prospects, but had woken to her choice of desirable jobs. She'd spent the morning fielding and returning calls, including a preliminary offer she'd just been made by the executives at the Fashion Channel.

"Another job offer?" Dylan asked.

He'd come home for lunch. Now he was preparing them both sandwiches. Lola had been assembling an accompanying salad, with the vegetables in his fridge, when the call came.

Lola nodded as she resumed chopping tomatoes. "The Fashion Channel wants me to host a model-themed reality show."

"That sounds interesting." Dylan cut both sandwiches on the diagonal. "I think you'd be great at it."

Lola nodded. "It does sound like fun, but it wasn't the most interesting call I received this morning."

Dylan raised a curious brow, and Lola, who was practically bursting, began to fill him in.

"Cole called shortly after you left to do your morning patrol. He wants me to consider a bigger role in the running of the company," she said. "He even sounded contrite."

"Your brother? Contrite?" Dylan chuckled as he slid a plate bearing a turkey sandwich across the breakfast bar in her direction. "I would like to have heard that conversation."

"I know. I nearly fell off my chair."

The phone rang again, but Lola ignored it. Dylan had come home for lunch to see her instead of eating at his mom's or the diner. Lola didn't know what the future held for them or if they even had one, so she didn't want to waste their precious time together talking on the phone.

She placed the finished salad at the center of the table. She was retrieving a bottle of salad dressing from the refrigerator when her phone began chirping, indicating she had both a voice mail and text message.

"I'll switch that off while we eat," she said.

"It's cool if you have business to handle," Dylan said.

She glanced at the clock on the microwave and then waggled her eyebrows at him. "If there's time after we eat, I've got some business for you to handle." She smacked his ass as she walked past him to get her phone.

"You'd better get your rest this afternoon," he called out to her retreating back. "Because I intend to handle that business all night long."

Picking up the phone, Lola immediately saw a text

message from her former agent on the locked screen. She shook her head and switched off the phone. She'd get back with Jill later.

"Problem?" Dylan asked.

"Not at all." Lola sat on a stool at the breakfast bar. "It was just my former agent asking for a second chance."

"Is that a possibility?" he asked, and then took a huge bite out of his sandwich.

Lola shrugged. "Anything's possible. It would largely depend on if she understood that she works for me, not vice versa. I won't tolerate being berated like a naughty child or disrespect from anyone. Not anymore."

Lola watched a smile form on his full lips. Dylan put down his sandwich, held up his fist, and she promptly bumped it with her own.

"Good job," he said.

She picked up her sandwich, and then placed it back on her plate. "Speaking of second chances," she said. "I've been thinking, and I believe Officer Wilson deserves another one."

Dylan's expression darkened. "He lied, Lola."

"I know, but…"

"No buts. A cop has to be aboveboard," Dylan said. "And how can you defend him after you nearly got arrested due to his nonsense?"

"Because I know how it feels to have people disrespect you, to treat you like a joke. He wanted to tell the truth, but was just afraid of once again being ridiculed as the bumbling rookie." Lola pleaded the young man's case.

"I'll think about it," Dylan said. "Meanwhile, you have bigger and better to things to think about than Todd Wilson. You have a huge career decision to make."

Lola exhaled and made a mental note to bring the subject up with Dylan at another time. She didn't have to think about her next career move. Lola already knew which job she truly wanted.

Her only question was did she have the guts to go for it?

Chapter 16

Lola left the next day.

Dylan had known something was up the moment he'd awakened. Usually, she was still asleep when he left the house to make his early-morning patrol through town. However, when his alarm had gone off, she had already showered and dressed.

Her suitcase was in the trunk of her red Mustang. She'd kissed him goodbye, told him she was Nashville bound and would be in touch.

He'd known all along this day would come. Still, he hadn't been prepared. It had taken every shred of strength he possessed to let her go, when everything in him wanted to take her back to bed and make love to her until she could barely stand, never mind leave.

"Chief?"

Dylan blinked. Marjorie was standing at his desk, staring at him curiously. "What's up?" he asked.

"I've been standing here talking to you a few minutes, but I don't think you've heard a word."

Dylan didn't bother denying it. He'd simply been going through the motions of his daily routine in the week since Lola had left Cooper's Place, his home and his bed. He apologized to the dispatcher and asked her to repeat what she'd said to him earlier.

"I was asking if you'd heard from Lola?" Marjorie cast a glance at the small-town police station's lone jail cell. The duvet, lampshade and other touches of pink reminiscent of the woman who'd occupied it for less than an hour.

Dylan nodded. Lola had kept her word about staying in touch. She'd called him when she'd made it back to Nashville, and two days later she'd phoned from New York. The last call had been a brief one from Los Angeles, where she was meeting with producers for a television show.

He hadn't heard from her last night or the night before. He'd expected her calls to eventually phase out. Dylan had thought about calling her. He'd picked up his phone at least a dozen times a day, his finger hovering over the number. Each time, he shoved the phone back into his pocket.

"She was only in town for a few days, but it's not the same around here without her." Marjorie shrugged. "I suppose we'll all get used to it."

Lola deserved each one of these opportunities. Dylan knew regardless of which one she decided to pursue, she'd excel. He wouldn't stand in her way. No matter how much he *liked* her. He found the corner of his mouth pull into a half smile as he remembered their private joke, always using the word *like* in lieu of the *L*-word that truly expressed their feelings.

"Chief?"

This time, Dylan heard Marjorie call him, and looked up in her direction. The dispatcher was frowning.

"Your uncle's on the phone. He sounds angry. Says to put you on the line ASAP."

"Ass," Dylan muttered under his breath. Once again he thought of how he and Lola said the word simultaneously whenever his uncle Roy's name came up.

Shake it off, man.

Dylan stood. "I'll walk over to city hall and see what he's upset about this time." Hopefully, the fresh air would clear his head of the woman dominating his thoughts.

He was nearly at the glass double doors leading out of the building when Rosemary Moody burst through it. "Have you heard the news?" she asked breathlessly.

Dylan frowned. "You know I don't listen to gossip, Rosemary," he said. "Why don't you give my mom a call? I'm sure she'll want to hear your news."

Having caught her breath, the older woman smiled smugly. "Oh, you're going to want to hear this gossip, Chief Cooper."

"I want to hear it," Marjorie yelled over his shoulder.

Shaking his head, Dylan walked around the town

busybody and pushed opened the door. He froze in the doorway, spotting Rosemary's big news at the same time she announced it.

"Lola's back, and she's just filed the paperwork to run for mayor!"

Dylan blinked, and his mouth stretched into a full-fledged grin.

Lola was leaning against her red Mustang, which was parked in front of the station. He walked over to the car, resisting the urge to break into a run. She smiled back at him. "I was on my way in to see you, but I didn't want to steal Rosemary's thunder."

"But you were in Nashville, and then New York and Los Angeles," he said, still stunned.

"I had my mind made up before I left, but I thought I owed it to myself to hear all the offers," she said. "And to tell my family personally I'd be voting my own shares of Espresso Cosmetics from now on, but I wouldn't be involved in the day-to-day operation of the company."

She handed him a sheaf of papers, and Dylan quickly thumbed through them. Rosemary was right. Lola Gray was officially a candidate for mayor of Cooper's Place.

"I used your address on the application. I hope you don't mind," she said.

"From now on it's our address, because I like you, Lola Gray. More than I've ever liked anyone in my entire life."

She smiled. "I like you, too, Dylan Cooper, and I

can't wait to get you home, strip that uniform off you and show you just how much."

He wrapped an arm around her waist and pulled her close, and then he captured her mouth in a kiss that left no doubt to how very deeply he liked her.

Dylan broke the kiss to take another look at the copy of the documents she'd filed. "I still can't believe it. You had your choice of the most glamorous places and careers in the world, and you're staying in town."

Lola threw her arms around his neck. "Baby, I'm staying to *run this town*."

Epilogue

Four months later

Wearing a simple white sheath with pearls adorning her ears and neck, Lola stood inside the gazebo in the Cooper's Place town square surrounded by friends and family.

"You look beautiful." Her father kissed her cheek. "I only wish your mother could be here today. She'd be so proud of you, and I believe she'd like your young man."

"I like him, too, Dad." She exchanged a look with Dylan, who was standing nearby. They'd been living together since her return to town, and she'd never been happier.

The ceremony was brief and tears welled in Lola's

eyes as she made an oath before God and everyone she held dear.

"Congratulations, Mayor Gray."

A beaming Lola shook hands with the judge who had just sworn her into office. Her second congratulations came from Dylan, who wasted no time sweeping her into his arms.

"You did such a good job painting this gazebo, I think we should hold another ceremony here," he said.

"Are you proposing to me, Chief Cooper?"

Dylan nodded as he pulled a small velvet box from his pocket. He opened it, revealing a diamond solitaire. "Well, what do you say?"

Lola grinned. "I think this town is about to have another mayor who goes by the name of Cooper."

* * * * *

SPECIAL EXCERPT FROM

HHARLEQUIN®

KIMANI
ROMANCE

*A teaching invitation gives Professor Donovan Boudreaux
the chance to meet his secret email pen pal. Renowned
author Gianna Martelli introduces him to the hidden
pleasures of Tuscany—and a surprise passion…*

Read on for a sneak peek at
TUSCAN HEAT, the next exciting installment in
Deborah Fletcher Mello*'s sensual series*
THE BOUDREAUX FAMILY*!*

Everyone in the room turned at the same time.
Gianna Martelli stood in the doorway, a bright smile
painting her expression. Donovan pushed himself up
from his seat, a wave of anxiety washing over him.
Gianna met his stare, a nervous twitch pulsing at the edge
of her lip. Light danced in her eyes as her gaze shifted
from the top of his head to the floor beneath his feet and
back, finally setting on his face.

Donovan Boudreaux was neatly attired, wearing a
casual summer suit in tan-colored linen with a white dress
shirt open at the collar. Brown leather loafers completed
his look. His dark hair was cropped low and close, and
he sported just the faintest hint of a goatee. His features
were chiseled, and at first glance she could have easily
mistaken him for a high fashion model. Nothing about

him screamed teacher. The man was drop-dead gorgeous, and as she stared, he took her breath away.

The moment was suddenly surreal, as though every-thing was moving in slow motion. As she glided to his side, Donovan was awed by the sheer magnitude of the moment, feeling as if he was lost somewhere deep in the sweetest dream. And then she touched him, her slender arms reaching around to give him a warm hug.

"It's nice to finally meet you," Gianna said softly. "Welcome to Italy."

Donovan's smile spread full across his face, his gaze dancing over her features. Although she and her sister were identical, he would have easily proclaimed Gianna the most beautiful woman he'd ever laid eyes on. The photo on the dust jacket of her books didn't begin to do her justice. Her complexion was dark honey, a sun-kissed glow emanating from unblemished skin. Her eyes were large saucers, blue-black in color, and reminded him of vast expanses of black ice. Her features were delicate, a button nose and thin lips framed by lush, thick waves of jet-black hair that fell to midwaist on a petite frame. She was tiny, almost fragile, but carried herself as though she stood inches taller. She wore a floral-print, ankle-length skirt and a simple white shirt that stopped just below her full bustline, exposing a washboard stomach. Gianna Martelli was stunning!

Don't miss
TUSCAN HEAT by Deborah Fletcher Mello,
available January 2016 wherever
Harlequin® Kimani Romance™
books and ebooks are sold.

REQUEST YOUR FREE BOOKS!

2 FREE NOVELS
PLUS 2 FREE GIFTS!

KIMANI™
ROMANCE

Love's ultimate destination!

KROM15